BALANCE

Kit White

Text © Kit White 2016
Cover Art and Design by Dale French

Kit White has asserted her right under the Copyright, Design and Patents Act 1988, to be identified as the author of this work.

All rights reserved.

No part of this publication may be reproduced or transmitted or utilized in any form or by any means, electronic, mechanical, photocopying or otherwise, without the prior permission of the publisher.

*For Christopher, my son.
With love.*

Artwork supplied by Dale French

CHAPTER 1

I weigh things.

After they've checked the offenders' packages to ensure they don't contain anything they shouldn't, they're weighed by Yours Truly. Not all packages are vetted, just those dispatched from the hard-core wing: the 90/91.

Maybe it's boredom? Maybe it's because I weigh those standard, rectangular browns one after the other, hour after hour, I'm beginning to think that life is a balancing act.

I can visualize my life bouncing up and down on those silver metal plates, negative, positive, up, down, up, down. Shit happens on one side, so I rebalance on the other. Easy? Not so much.

That's why I'm here. Welcome to HMYOI Hendbrook.

Sometimes, I imagine that big American statue, what's her name? Liberty! She's standing there and worrying about that robe draping precariously over her shoulder, pinned for virtue; will it, won't it fall? Will it, won't it tip those scales?

Crazy thoughts! But that's what happens when you stand all day weighing packages and grapple with the fact that you've screwed up big time.

Sure, we actually have the old-fashioned scales with weights, but we've got the neat minute digitals too.

Listen up! This is a new complex for the rehabilitation of today's young offenders: like, all the bells and whistles, man. Aren't we the lucky ones! But I kind of don't mind using the seesaws, watching those metal arms rise and dive. They make me think. Maybe that's what my key-worker, Mr Armstrong, planned when he suggested I volunteer to work in the post room. "Good to show an interest in things, young man," he'd advised. "The better the behaviour inside, the better fixed you are for appeal and an early out."

I guess he thought YT would meditate seriously on his criminal behaviour; he would weigh up his life, repent and rebalance the scales.

But read on. Here it is, all down in my journal; at least I owe her that, the precious giver of this gift.

Yours Truly – aka Lawrence.

OK. So, YT's not my real name, obviously. My other label is Bounce. I'm Bounce to my proper mates on the outside, 'cause of the Parkour: the jumps. I can bounce all right: rooftop-to-rooftop. Bounce is to the mates I grew up with, the ones I stepped out of school and joined the world of grown-ups with. My mates christened me Bounce when I took a jump none of them could master and then celebrated, putting back the cider in a cloud of smoke from the wacky backy.

I've got a bit of a bounce in my step too, I don't drag my heels, I've got to keep moving. Can't stand still, like, if I do, something lurking out there, some ominous presence is going to grab me and if it doesn't beat the shit out of me, it'll lock

BALANCE

me in some concrete box, for good. Yeah? Too late! Locked up and yet I still need to keep moving. I bounce down the corridors like frickin Tigger.

I've also got a black curly lock of hair that falls over my forehead. My mum used to pull it gently then watch it bounce back up. Like it was some amazing trick, ta dah! But I guess she thought I was: my very existence was the amazing trick, some great achievement, her criminal son. Back then, I was her bouncy little miracle.

Like I say, strange connections in the brain when you're inside. Mum still tugged that curl when I was fourteen, like I was still her innocent baby boy, sad, sad!

Inside Her Majesty's, I'm 'Shithead' to the hardcore guys I pass on the way to the canteen. I don't disown that name, for obvious reasons. You don't mess with the hardcore 90/91 offenders then they won't mess with you. Yeah, it can kind of get nasty in here and the thing is, you never know which way the shit's heading and where exactly it's coming from. But you develop an internal sensor, if you're lucky. A basic savage instinct resurfaces. It's something that's probably been dormant for thousands of years, like when we needed to know where the sabretooth was hanging out, ready to pounce and tear you to pieces, man, or if our cave neighbour's spear was aimed right on target. Only, in this place you don't see the spears – you see the scars.

My sensor hit the on switch pretty quick when I arrived: when it's fired up, it rises to the surface of my skin, making the hairs stand on end as it picks up that charge in the air.

But, if you're unlucky, like Herbert was, then you're a prime target and hit the medical centre, cutting and burning your flesh and begging the medics to keep you hidden, out of sight, forever. Yeah, Herbert, he's not wired right for this place, that's a cert.

"S'cuse, can I?" Herbert's standing here, hunched over his laundry sack, looking like he wants to pee. Only thing is, there's room here for twenty to cruise by.

"No worries, man," I say, like I'm the keeper of the invisible gate. I nod him on. Herbert shakes his white-blonde head, deferential like, poor camouflage when he came in, that, and the terror in his eyes means the guy still looks like a real baby, and was labelled 'sucker' on his arrival.

Herbert shuffles past, his eyes darting anxious glances in my direction like I'm about to leap on him and rip him to pieces; I am the sabretooth.

I give him some distance before wandering down at snail's pace to the scrubs.

I'm 'My Darling', to Officer Pevensey. So here I am and here she is holding out my clean towels and fresh toiletries for the changes this week. Su-weet!

"Hello, my darling, how's my Heathcliff doing?" she asks and smiles like she's won the jackpot and not the shitpot.

"I'm good, thanks," and I beam back.

"Not so good, darling, or you wouldn't be here," she chuckles and her whole, wholesome body wobbles under the exertion.

"Yeah," I agree, and I know she's used that line before.

I almost started to fancy her, the chunky Officer Pevensey. She's fifty-something and smiling at me with her crinkling upturned pixie nose, wrinkling her pale blue eyes

BALANCE

and shaking her bottle-red, badly cut hair. She seriously needs to sort her hairdresser out.

Luca the Latvian stomps round the corner wearing his shades. He's probably not Latvian, or any other Vian for that matter, but when you get a name in here, it kind of hangs.

Luca thinks he's Bond.

"Morning, Luca," Pevensey's looking at his laundry bag and indicates to the chute. Luca lunges over, tips up the bag and watches its contents slide away. He flicks the empty sack in the air, like it's some friggin party trick and he's hot to trot. Only Luca's about as far from cool dude as you can get. He's big, sure! But he's clumsy, and its like he's got twenty fat fingers on each hand and he lollops down the corridors trying to be smooth, easy, sophisticated, but he's just one big Frankenstein.

"Thanks," I say to Pevensey as I make my retreat, but suddenly Luca is shoulder-to-shoulder, "O.P's got nice ones," he announces, within her earshot. Thanks for that, Luca! I glance back at her, partly to see if she's heard and to reassess her shapely frame and OK she has big boobs that her navy fleece battles daily to contain, like the inmates here. It displays the establishment insignia in bright yellow letters right over her left breast like it's some kind of fashion statement.

Luca's eyes are locked hard on her, like he's fighting yet can't draw his gaze away from them!

Pevensey doesn't rate him, I can see, but she flashes me a wink as I head away. Yeah, and I can still hear her, trotting about in the laundry room when I'm halfway down the hall.

She jangles when she walks does Officer Pevensey: jingle-jangle the keys to the linen stores. Jingle- jangle the keys

KIT WHITE

to your dreams. Yeah! Get it? I was kind of suffering from Luca's problem too. I had actually started to dream about Pevensey doing a hula dance with the clinking keys on her hips: hundreds and hundreds of jangling keys just gyrating down the corridor.

Then I realised it was more of a nightmare than a dream. I woke up in a sweat. I was losing my head, seriously losing perspective. Gross! Like, she's old enough to be my mum and when did my dreams of the gorgeous eighteen-year-old, Lily, my last love interest, who used to smile so temptingly when I bought my beers at the local kiosk, disappear?

Here's that scenario – she dropped me down to zero when I was charged with GBH. In all honesty I'm not about to blame her. It's just tough.

Yeah – the scales dived right to the base when that text beeped in: "I love you. But we're history. You're bad news. How could you do that to someone? Lil."

Cheers for that, Lil. But I get where you're coming from. Then I wonder, to be fair, would I wait for her if she'd been sent down for GBH? Come to think of it, no way would Lil commit a GBH, so that's a no-goer.

Weird wonderings! Life's questions, life's fantasies fusing with realities, sparking the electrodes in my brain until it feels like it's about to short-circuit.

I've been inside for eighteen months. By the time you add on the remanding in custody and pending hearing and youth assessments, it'll be nearly three years. Three years!

"Hey, Lawrence." Walter's standing there with that inane grin on his face like he's a Happy Chappy and really pleased to be here. He's talking and chirping at me like a wrinkly out for a morning stroll. His red and white striped beanie doesn't do him any favours either.

"Right!" I rub my eyes and hope when I look back, the where's Wally's disappeared.

No joy!

He's bulging out of his blue sweatshirt and when he turns to peer down the corridor at some monkeying noises echoing up to us, I can see the crack in his arse; his trousers are almost to his knees, man. Style's OK, but give a boy a break!

"What time are you going to the canteen, Lawrence?" he asks like he's fixing us up.

Uh! No, I don't think so.

"Don't know, man. Don't hang around for me, not sure what the plan is today," I say quickly. I'm not into making commitments, even if it is for a shit lunch in the mess hall.

Walter's sweating already; his big moon face is shiny and red, resembling the flowers he grows.

I've got to tell you, time has not flown. Time's taken a real dislike to YT. It's been dragging its fat, flesh-flapping, ugly heels right past my cell door: time and Walter Anderson.

Walter's in for growing cannabis and he's as obese and ugly and slow as time. Only Walter grew the leaf so prolifically, he would have put the farmers of Columbia to shame. He grew the green so good that he made a lot of friends: real buddies. But Walter's a bit dim; when he was sent down, he couldn't figure out why his mates didn't come to visit on a regular basis. Like he seriously believed that he was the magnet man, not the green?

Walter drags his flabby carcass past my door every morning at six a.m., depressed and depressing. I imagine time, a physical being, a dwarf-like creature sitting on Walter's shoulder and waving at me as the sad bastard shuffles past with his stupid watering can; they both irritate the shit out of me: Walter and time.

Walter's pretty harmless; it's time that's the killer.

"Mr Hobbs says I grow the best bromeliads he's ever seen," announces Walter, with a cocky grin.

"No kidding? Sounds like, prehistoric. Like it should have wings, or horns," I say.

Walter chuckles.

"No, seriously, that's cool man, Walter. I can't grow peanuts. Yeah, it's good to have gift."

"Peanuts? No way! That's what I tried to grow. You peel the shell, shove them in good dirt and they take off. No kidding. Thing is, you've gotta get the non-roasted, Lawrence, or they don't peg," says Walter, like I know what the hell he's talking about and I'm even interested.

"OK, I'll bear that in mind," I say, tongue in cheek and shoving my stuff around the desk to think about nothing. "Guess I'm talking to the expert."

Walter grins. "Yeah, I'll grow some nuts sometime and you'll see," he says.

That'd be a plan, Walter," I reply, unable to resist the smile it brings to my face.

I wave a farewell and he trots away with his watering can.

I know it's tough in here and every little helps us get through the day, so I'm not about to piss on Walter's peanut parade. Why would I?

But here's the strange twist of fate, get this: the youth rehabilitation officer on our wing has given Walter his own garden. There's irony! Walter's got green fingers all right. He was doing just fine and dandy at the college on an Agriculture Foundation Course until he got the Midas touch.

I quote Walter, on his arrival: 'Students have the opportunity to complete a number of projects in a practical environment, man," Walter recited. "Hey, I would have got A* on my leaves, like the best smoke you'd ever have. Everyone said I was class A." Yeah, and he was proud as punch; he laughed himself stupid.

Sad, isn't it? He actually thinks it's clever to grow thousands of pounds worth of cannabis and be ripped off by his 'mates'.

Walter was just the worker bee and as he nurtured his beautiful plants his popularity grew when he gave the leaf away.

He worked for friendship, acceptance, and in the end the loser got time.

After Walter's arrest, his friendships withered on the vine. But his sentence is pretty short. He'll be out soon, lucky boy.

I suppose you think I'm hard; I should feel sorry for the butthead.

Sorry! No way.

I don't like stupidity in any form, especially my own, and I don't feel sorry for me, so why the shit should I feel bad for him?

After Walter's left my space I get up and slam my door. Bang!

I'm pissed off, man, sick of the inane grins, the jokes echoing down the corridors, the constant reminders I'm with company I don't want to keep. So I shut out that I am in.

It never works and I just get fired up and end up pacing my room like some animal at the zoo.

So, Walter's got a slap on the hand for growing and I've got three years for GBH. My label sticks man: it's burnt into the skin, painfully seared through my flesh like a brand.

I go to my desk and fiddle with the bundle of letters she's sent. I lift it up and it becomes that stone in my chest: making it hard for me to breathe.

I grip it, tighter.

I wonder, should I bin it, the whole friggin lot? Like throwing that stone into the sea, casting it away forever.

But I put the bundle down beside the other piles and the stone sinks deep inside for the millionth time.

OK, so the story is, my mother and father christened me Lawrence in our local church when they believed an angel had fallen into their arms.

Mum's still got the photos hanging round the house of the young marrieds with a white lace bundle in their arms.

Well, let me explain in the first instance that not everyone in this dump is from a 'bad' home. I went to a good school. Believe it or not, there was a time when I liked thinking, but the proper thinking: working out maths and science projects and – yeah, I used to get a kick out of getting it right and discovering things.

Mum's still got a lot of my writing too. I found them in a box on top of her wardrobe when she asked me to put her old nursing kit up there.

That was a sad, sad day. I remember the look on her face; it's etched into my brain and that picture won't ever fade.

BALANCE

My English book with all my old stories, bio and poetry work from year seven, was sticking out of the box.

"Jeeze, Mum, why have you got this stuff?" I'd asked in disgust, blowing off the dust and crap.

She was standing, her hair wrapped up in that big flower scrunchy that she wore year after year, but it never worked, she constantly flicked her hair out of her eyes and that was when I saw how sad she was, but not just sad, it was deeper, more painful. It hurt me, just seeing it.

"Oh, Lawrence, when you were little, your work was hilarious. I often went through your books and chuckled at the things you said. There's one you've written about you and Harriet buying a gum factory and making boeuf bourguignon, chicken pâté and all these ridiculous flavours just for grown-ups and there was even fishcake gum. Oh and the wine, you decided you'd open a shop called Gum on the Go for adults. You were both going to be millionaires."

It all came back, in that instant, how Harrie had snatched the book from my hand and helped me with my English homework. It had degenerated into chaos as it always did with Harrie, the science projects, the models. I was closer to Harrie than anyone else in my life. I glanced at the box of books and scraps and resisted the temptation to take it down and relive Mum's happier days with her.

I'd wished I hadn't asked. I took her kit bag from her arms and silently shoved it up on top of the cabinet.

Shit happens. I knew I'd be out again that same day, pissing about and that was what I'd become – one big piss-take.

So clever little me at school, from a good home, full of ideas, potential, until... as my parents tried to explain to the nice officer gentleman, I merely fell into 'bad' company. There's not a 'bad' bone in my body.

The fact that my actions broke nearly every bone in someone else's body still doesn't make me bad in my mother's eyes.

My father takes a different angle. He just thinks I'm a loser. Fair play.

But get this, the old man's a shit too and I don't mean a wife-beating, drunk kind of shit. No way! He's not out there; he's under the covers: a smarter, cleaner, respectable kind of shit. He plays the field, takes the piss.

Mum's stuck by him for years, handling all the boring shit while Mr Ego's been screwing the skirts. I rarely saw him: he kind of swept in, got what he needed, then cruised out of our lives again.

And, as the years ticked on, Mum just held it all together.

So, hurting someone who's hurt you is fair play, evening the odds, that's on the level. But not dumping on her like that.

She's not stupid either, that's what makes it worse: the humiliation. He's been out there with skirts nearly as young as my big sis: making Mum the local joke.

Sad, man.

But Mum kind of made her decision way back. She stuck it out and now, I guess, she reckons two parts to two parts makes it her investment, me and Harrie.

But I wish she hadn't.

Harrie may have been worth it. But not me, no way.

So, cracking on to my next broken relationship – big sis. Harriet?

Well get this, she tipped off the police and tipped those scales to the negative big time.

BALANCE

The statement Harrie gave in court sent me plummeting and I don't think I'm ever going to come up again.

No, Harrie destroyed her kid brother.

"Hey, Postman Pat, it's canteen Funday, today." My mate, Lewis, sticks his head round the door and tosses some screwed up paper at me. He's beaming sunshine.

"You – pick that up." That's L. James, our warden. He's ex-army. He's seen things not even the hardcore 90/91 have seen. He says he's seen things in the call of duty that would make us vomit; the fallout from bombs, bits of bodies and shit like that.

He doesn't think we're so cool, so tough. He just thinks we're silly little boys.

He's OK, I suppose, but if you get on the wrong side of L. James, then life is a real bummer.

I saw the might of L. James' power the day Stu had Herbert up against a wall. "Oy, Ridman, what the hell are you playing at?" L. James hollered.

He hammered down the corridor like a beast for Ridman.

"Herby owes me, don't you, Herby?'

Stu released Herby's collar and Herby sagged down against the wall. Herby shoved his glasses back onto his nose and kept his head down.

"You're lying," said L. James.

Herby started blubbing with the shakes.

"He owes me," Stu, said, making a fist.

"I'm not listening,' said L. James.

I watched as L. James closed the gap.

I guessed the boss to be around the forty-something mark; Stu was nineteen, fit, beefy and ready to take him out.

13

"This is none of your shitting business. This is for me and him to sort," snarled Stu.

Stu flexed his arms and jabbed his finger into Herby's gut, inciting L. James to act.

Herby grunted with each prod, but never raised his arms from his side to protect himself.

I could see Stu wanted to take L. James down. He wasn't interested in the scrawny Herb any more. No, now he was going to prove to everyone on the floor that he was ahead of L. James in the fearing ranks.

"What are you in for, Ridman? Can you remember?" asked L. James, calm, steady. He was wearing navy chinos with the radio wire hanging out of his pocket, but I could see, no way was he intending to reach for it. He knew if he did, things would escalate and Ridman would be locked down in solitary.

"You know what I'm in for, it's on record and I can do it again."

Stu stepped up and shoved L. James back.

Then he waited, grinning, hoping for the kick-off.

L. James came back at him. His voice was low, sincere. "Don't push your luck, Ridman. I know what's going on with your little lad, but what's the point of proving to your kid that you're nothing but a brainless bully? So, you can beat the shit out of Herbert. What does that prove to your kid? Having a son's a big deal. If you want to see him again, you need to grow up."

A small group of us gathered round. I could see some were itching for the fight: a bit of action to break up the monotony and a battle between Ridman and L. James would

BALANCE

have been match of the week. I was pitching for L. James to flatten Stu; after all, the guy was a bullying dick.

"My kid's got nothing to do with you." Ridman's face flushed up. I could see him clenching his fists but there was a flash of panic.

"No! You're right, 'cause it's not me your girlfriend's blocking, is it? He's what, three now? How many times has he seen you since he was born? Once? Twice? Nah, it's not my business and frankly I don't give a shit if your son never sees you again. But it is your business and you'd better clean it up or he'll forget about you, Ridman. He won't even know your name by the time you get out if you don't toe the line."

Christ! Suicide, L. James. I stood waiting for Ridman to spill his blood all over the hall floor, like I couldn't believe that anyone would have the balls to say that to Ridman.

Ridman's got pictures of his kid pinned to his locker in the gym and I'd heard that when some airhead drew a tache on one photo, Ridman put the sucker in plaster for three months.

L. James went right for Ridman's nerve. Bullseye!

Doors slammed, echoing reminders that time was passing as we all stood round waiting for action.

Ridman glared back, his mind whirling. I watched his eyes darting from the sniffling Herb to L. James.

He froze, trapped. He didn't know which way to move, he was weighing up the odds, how'd he come out of this one? We'd all been there, all done it, the balancing act.

"Come on, your kid doesn't want this and I want my bloody break," snapped L. James.

It was enough.

Ridman stepped back and L. James relaxed. I watched his shoulders drop as he waved Herby on.

Herby sidled along the wall, then hammered down the hall to his room, followed by taunts and jeers.

Then the disappointed audience cracked at the edges and broke away, bemoaning the waste of time.

I turned to go, but then I saw it, for a fleeting second. Ridman, he's rubbing his eyes, yeah, like he's battling not to cry.

Ridman? Tragic!

L. James – Respect!

But not me, man, I don't cry in public. I just don't get on the wrong side of L. James. As simple as!

Now, L. James is giving Lewis the evils while I shove the last pile of browns into the band and then bag them.

"Whoops, sorry, sir." Lewis grabs up the paper and shoves it in his pocket, amiably and politely. See? Sometimes being a tough bastard works.

It's the weekend. We all get to choose how long we're in the canteen for and there's even a menu. It's a bit like going out for the day, only on the inside, if you get my meaning.

Anyway, we kind of linked up early on, Lewis and me. He's sharp; he's funny and he's unlucky, that's all. He's also got a thing about motors and speed and danger is his hit.

I told him, "You should have joined the army and become a tank driver."

"Yeah, maybe. But I like going out where and when I like, not where and when I'm told," he'd said. I get the point. Only now he can't go out at all for another year.

BALANCE

He's done six months. He caused some serious damage to public property by driving a Subaru four- wheel straight through the entrance of the closed shopping mall at one in the morning. He and his mates went late-night shopping. They drove all the way down the mall: past the water fountains, the escalators, the flower displays and the seated areas.

Now, there's window-shopping for you!

Lewis said it was like something out of a film, or a kick-ass speedway game.

By the time they decided to turn round and drive back out, coppers had blocked every exit.

That's not unlucky: I get that. That's criminal, what Lewis did.

But the unlucky part is that he'd decided to give up the boy racer, carjacker life for good. He had plans; he had a job and a love interest. This was to be his grand finale, his Subaru song. He'd been doing it since he was thirteen and the driving was all getting a bit jaded. He'd never been caught, never had a record, he was clean and sparkling. He was in with a chance.

He might have got a lighter sentence if he hadn't broken a copper's leg on the way out with the back of his four-wheel.

Unlucky!

But when he's out, he can move on, rebuild, be a better boy. Point is, Lewis wasn't betrayed, no one pointed the finger and said, send him down.

Betrayal, that's what eats away at the soul, destroys the spirit.

So sure, Lewis was unlucky, but just unlucky.

CHAPTER 2

I am not unlucky. I am a spoilt little shit. I know, because Dad told me when he came to visit one Sunday.

Mum just stiffened up and sat with her back rigid, fiddling with her skirt in that irritating, it won't sit right fashion. I resisted hammering my fist on the table in anger and gave in to pity. But she smiles at me, like everything's hunky dory while the old man stares, boring his hate and contempt into my skin.

It's all 'only family matters' to her, keeping things good, pleasant, normal.

I've known about the old man's flings for years now. Ever since I found a little love note under the driver's seat of Dad's car.

I told him I knew. I waved the note under his nose and you know what? There was nothing but lies, all the time, lies.

First he raised his fist, like he was going to lay one on me. Then he realised the boy might be thirteen and a half, but he can sock him back and just as hard. So his fist hung like a hammer in the air, but it didn't come down, man, no way.

BALANCE

Next came the long, aggrieved stare as he explained that things weren't as they seemed and life's not all black and white and to just butt out of his business.

He said things had been bad for a long time between him and Mum and how this latest woman had actually saved his marriage.

Yeah, right! Her and the others he'd obviously been screwing over the years. He was never there, never with us. It all added up.

Tosser!

Anyway, I wasn't about to shatter Mum's illusion of happy families, was I? She'd have been crushed if she thought I knew about all that crap. It was the hiding that made it impossible for me to bring it up. I wasn't sure if she was pushing it all out of sight, or if she genuinely didn't know.

So now I just look at her and look at him and don't think about the mess.

I know I've let Mum down, but I know I care about her and I wouldn't screw her over like he's done.

Somehow, I'll make it up to her, somehow.

"So, is that what you've come to tell me then, Dad? What a spoilt little shit I am?" I asked, after he'd pushed for the millionth time for me to see Harrie and how desperate she is to visit. I refused.

"I've come to tell you to at least read your sister's letters and scribble some semblance of a reply. "Things are changing in her life, Lawrence. Things you should know about, yet you won't let her visit and now you don't even have the decency to answer her notes. It's breaking her heart," said Dad.

19

"Keep them to yourself, Dad, or I'm out of here. Anyway, it doesn't add up, does it? She signed the statement that put me in here." I shrugged, job done.

"You put you in here, no one else. That man has to walk with crutches possibly for the rest of his life because of your vicious, moronic behaviour. You were just looking for an excuse to be the big man. Harriet never asked you to put Rich in hospital. She just told the police what she saw," Dad informed me, with his usual contempt.

"Look, we're going round in circles here. Why not give yourselves a break and take off for the day? I've got things to do and you don't want to waste your time with me," I'd said, and I actually meant it. Goodbye and good riddance.

I stood up.

"That's it with you, isn't it, Lawrence? Never been clever enough to talk things through – just walk away from problems. Hurt, that's all you're capable of, hurt," started Dad.

"Yeah? Don't push me on that one," I replied, and he knew just what I was talking about.

You see, when you've got ammo like his affairs, it's like gold. Dad's face set in anger and I saw Mum reach across and squeeze his arm.

"Please, can't we just spend a few minutes together without bickering? We only get a brief visit. We won't mention Harriet again. But she's doing fine. I thought you'd like to know that, Lawrence..." Mum's words trailed.

So I sat and dutifully listened to the daily pains and pleasures of family and neighbours and thought what a criminal waste of a Saturday afternoon and if only...

CHAPTER 3

Sunday, Sunday, my favourite day.

I never used to like Sundays, not before I was in here. Sundays were for visiting pews and prayers hanging empty in the air. Mum she churched it come hell or high water. Hallelujah!

For me, they were dead days, empty, closed, quiet nothingness and there was the prospect of Monday and the fact that I hadn't done any essays or other work to hand in at school because I'd spent Sunday smoking spliffs and chilling with the mates.

I drifted into floating through life and never noticed when I floated out of my old life.

Soon, it didn't matter if it was Sunday because it merged with Monday and that's when I really lost it. Is it January or July?

Who gives a shit?

That's when Harrie began to hunt me down.

She'd text: You're a fourteen-year-old selfish shit: grow up. Mum's worried. When are you coming home?

My text: --

Her text: Where the hell are you?

My text: --

Her text: You'd better sort your life out, Lawrence.

She'd keep texting and I'd keep blanking. Well, you get the gist.

I guess, when I think back, Harrie missed me. No, it wasn't just about Mum or Dad. Harrie was screwed up too.

Harrie would rock up and meet me on my way back from school on her bike. Yeah, I loved that.

She'd roar round the corner in her leathers and we'd take off, anywhere and everywhere; beach, the old lead mines; one time, we biked for miles, pulled up and ate hotdogs as we watched the moon laying its yellow line across the water.

That was one of the rare times Harrie broke down on me. She'd had a blazer with Rich and she'd talked at me, told me stuff I didn't want to hear, but I'd listened.

And on the level, I wanted her back with him. He was a good guy, he made her happy and I liked to see her happy. I said to her, 'You can be a real bitch, Harrie, give him a break."

So yeah, the drifting, the floating away, I guess I stopped liking thinking and went for the forgetting.

Harrie's four years older than me. She does OK. She's clever, nice, attentive, a hard worker and university stuff. Harrie's everything a parent could want in a daughter and if I was someone else, she'd be everything I could want in a sister. But I'm not someone else. I'm me. I'm in this shithole and I'll never forgive her for sending me here.

Harrie knows. She sent me down. It's over.

"Go on, sod off, you're on short shift today, Lawrence," says L. James, giving me the evils, only I know he's being friendly like.

"Thanks, sir," I say. I do appreciate it. He sort of likes me in a 'you're no trouble and at least you have a few brain cells kind of way.

"Back here six forty-five tomorrow, Lawrence," he commands.

"On the dot, sir, cross my heart," I pledge as I tail Lewis out of the post room.

It's raining hard outside, battering on the new roof like it's made of tin. But it's strangely sunny and even stranger – my spirits are high. The rich, golden light is blasting through the streams of rain, forcing me to smile.

We head down to the canteen and I can smell the roasts wafting up the corridor. It's almost like being at school again; I have a fleeting feeling of carefree abandon, a childish optimism.

It passes as quickly as the Neanderthal who shoves me on his way to the canteen, making me collide with and bounce Lewis off of the wall.

Lewis glares at the back of Neanderthal's head, we exchange disgusted looks, but he holds his temper. Like me, Lewis knows the less you're riled in here, the quicker you get loose and the sweeter life is.

"How come you work in the post room and I don't get any letters?" asks Lewis.

" 'Cause nobody loves you, arse face."

I smile, remembering the first time I met Lewis when I was first locked up. Some guy had lifted a pack of tobacco from some shaved's seat when he'd wandered off for a conflab with another inmate in the rec room.

When Shave returned to find his baccy pack missing, he flipped. He kicked chairs, tossed tables and shit about, then he went for an all-out assault on Lewis, who'd been minding his own.

Shave was built like the Hulk and Lewis was no match, but respect, Lewis stood his ground.

"You! Give it back," hollered Shave.

"What, man?" Lewis stood in his 'come fly with me' teeshirt and put is hands in the air, "Seriously, what's your problem?"

"If you don't give me my pack, I'm going to rip your throat out," warned Shave.

I looked at Lewis, then I looked at Shave and concluded, there's only going to be one winner here: Lewis is history.

I was going to mind my own, but then Shave decided he'd provide some extra theatre by pulling off his leather belt and wrapping it round each fist for a total wipe-out.

"Hey, steady on," protested Lewis. "Look, mate, I wouldn't be stupid enough to lift anything from you."

"No?" said Shave, then he announced to the assembled crowd, "Whoever took my pack, drop it, or shit features gets the noose."

Lewis picked up a metal chair. He held it, legs forward, as if taming a wild bear, which, come to think of it, he kind of was.

"Look, man, I didn't take your pack," said Lewis.

He backed away, gripping the chair, but there was no fear, no panic in his eyes.

If it had been me, I'd have been shitting bricks.

"I don't care if you did, or if you didn't," said Shave, calmly. "Anyone takes anything from me, you're the one that gets it." Shave shrugged his shoulders

"Hey, I reckon he took it," said Lewis, pointing his finger at some guy pissing himself laughing at the prospect of some free wrestling.

"Yeah? Well, he'll get it after you then, won't he?" said Shave.

Shave lurched forward and Lewis prodded at him with the chair. Shouts and claps rang out as they danced around the mulberry bush until Shave released the buckle end of his belt and whiplashed Lewis.

Ouch! The metal cut deep.

"Shit!" Lewis dropped the chair and grabbed the top of his arm as blood leaked through his fingers and down to his wrist.

Shave flicked up the belt, wrapped it back around his hand and went in for the kill. That's when I decided, if I ever had to share a space with Shave or Lewis, which animal would it be?

I leapt at Shave and he rammed me into the wall, knocked the wind out of me.

Everyone was yelling and laughing, then some clever dick set the alarms ringing and everyone started legging it. Lewis leapt across and grabbed Shave's leg. Shave kicked out and laid one right on my mouth. I tell you, the pain surged up into my nose and I staggered, head ringing, waiting for the bells to end. Lewis tried to bring Shave down but the guy was made of steel, he wouldn't bend.

That's when Shave shoved me back and wrapped the belt round Lewis' head.

I heard Lewis gurgling beneath Shave's shoulders before the uniforms descended and sent the three of us crashing across the rec room and into a heap.

We were checked in first aid. I thought my ribs had been broken and every one of my teeth smashed out, but miraculously they survived, not even a crook. But when I stood up, I yelped with the stab in my chest.

The orderly checked me out, poking and prodding and declared me fit for duty and not damaged enough to warrant an X-ray. Thanks!

They glued Lewis' arm and put tape over it then we were all marched to solitary to cool down until cocoa time. Yeah, that's what they said, 'cocoa time'.

"That glue's wonder stuff," L. James remarked, when I told him next morning. "Army wouldn't be without it. They can stick anything these days. The wife uses it for everything. Reckon she puts it on the toilet seat, she's on the bloody thing long enough." He laughed.

So, some days later, Lewis got a pass and came knocking on my door.

He was the first and only inmate I ever invited into my cell.

"Hey, thanks, man," he said, wandering in and lying on my nicely made bed.

"Yeah, no worries, the film was shit anyway," I replied. "Boots off, man."

Lewis laughed, then dug down into his pocket and pulled out a pack of tobacco. "Hey, guess what I found in my pocket? Been keeping it for a celebration. The dick always takes from the squirts anyway. So it's payback. Want some?"

Class!

So here we are, nearly a year later and the sun's shining and we're still in one piece.

"You get letters all the time and you don't even open them," says Lewis and I can see he's genuinely puzzled. "Christ, you're cuckoo! She must have pissed you off big time."

"Who?"

"The bird who keeps writing!" Lewis looks at me as if I'm insane. "The one you've stacked all the letters on your desk from."

I shrug. "She's not my bird, she's my sister and I don't need her letters. I don't need anything from her." I try not to sound bitter, but that's the way I spit it out.

"OK, you're just collecting them, man, to use as arse rags."

I shrug. "Something like that."

"Not my business," says Lewis, resigned.

"No."

Walter's sitting with the younger group at the end of the canteen; he always gravitates towards the shrimps. I guess that's where he's accepted and feels safe, until a warden chases him back to the big boys' tables.

We're chilled. We sit with our full trays and I see there's a prism; the sun is beaming through the windows and cutting colours down through Lewis' glass of water. It hits the table in lines of pinks and purples and yellows. It's stunning: a natural beauty, forcing its way in.

Lewis sees it too.

"Nice," he observes.

I nod as I soak up the colours of something, spontaneous, fresh.

It's like something alive has the power to blast its purity right through the bleak, shatterproof windows and crush the darkness inside.

Blues, red and purples dance across our table-top, hypnotic!

We've agreed to get digs together when Lewis comes out. His release date is long after mine, so it's down to me to get the rooms sorted. I noticed a distinct change in Lewis' mood when we reached that agreement. Yes, I can say he's been a whole lot happier with that plan. I have too. I can't ever go back. My home's not an option – Harrie's there.

"Listen, man, I lived in a hole on the Cedar estate in London. There was a frickin stabbing in the area at least once a week."

"Where are your older brothers?" I'd asked, when I could see he was OK to talk.

"Nick's in the forces and Jamie drifted off to Scotland. He doesn't bother his arse to keep in touch. My folks are old, I mean ancient and a bit decrepit; they couldn't cope with any of us. I was the straw that broke the camel's, yeah? They just wanted me off their hands, so I obliged by taking a joyride."

The thing I discovered about Lewis is that he's absolute. There's a toughness in Lewis that sits right at the core.

Nothing screws him up, not like it does me.

His folks don't write, they don't visit; it's him alone against the world and yet he's OK with that. He says he understands they care, but can't cope; so he handles it. I respect that.

BALANCE

"Windows! We need digs with windows, man, especially after being cooped up in here," says Lewis, between crunches.

"We've got lots of windows in here," I say, glancing out.

"Yes, but they're different windows, aren't they? They're not ordinary windows; they're for monkeys in zoos," says Lewis.

I gaze across the canteen to the glass. It's thick and unyielding, encasing us in a shatterproof box that runs from ceiling to floor. It faces out onto an exercise and basketball court encircled by a concrete wall. The design's shit, for sure.

"OK, I get your point. I was thinking about somewhere up north, Newcastle maybe. There's work there." I can't stop beaming at the thought. Life's sweet sometimes, because it can be different; it doesn't have to be the here and now.

I like thinking about the future, but only when it means I don't waste the moment thinking about returning home to face Harrie and the domestic carnage from the old man. Somewhere in the back of my mind something's brewing, an idea about Mum. But it's got to be handled right, timing has to be good.

"Great call. Newcastle, man, that's nice. You've only got a short time left now, you lucky bastard."

I can see envy in his eyes.

There's a shark. It's cruising. Liam Woods is strolling towards us. He's been in these establishments since he was potty trained and that's the only training he's ever had. He spends most of his incarceration in the ISU on Howard wing. He's a machine.

I watch a whole body of trouble heading our way.

I straighten up.

"What's up?" Lewis' eyes dart in panic. In this place you only relax on the surface; you stay alert, primed.

Lewis glances over his shoulder, then turns back and sets his head down, concentrating hard on the shape of his plate. He waits for whatever's coming.

Woods is moving – oh so slowly. The canteen's noisy: dishes, cutlery, boisterous, rowdy crowds. The noise is growing in my head, painful throbbing. I can hear my heart begin to pump, whoosh, whoosh in my ears above the chaos.

I should be used to this. I should be confident, in control. But I'm not. It's like a new challenge: a new weight ready to tip those scales one way or the other.

I look across at Lewis as Woods' stinking combat trousers halt right beside our table.

He carries the stench of stale tobacco and sweat. Woods rests his tattooed hands on the surface and peers down at us.

"Afternoon, ladies," he quips. His narrow grey eyes lock on to me, rock solid.

Then he glances around to place the wardens and smiles amiably: like he's having a friendly chat with his best mates.

He's a real showman, is Woods.

"You're just a couple of queenies, aren't ya?" he announces.

I feel my arms tense into steel rods, ready.

"You've got friends, Woods. No one pushes you," Lewis says, trying to be easy.

Woods sniggers. "There's friends and there's," he purses his lips and kisses the air, "friends."

"Clown," I say to Lewis under my breath.

But my intestines are contracting and twisting as my gut muscles tighten the coils.

BALANCE

My relaxed lunch is beginning to turn to lead in my belly.

"Which one's the gardener?" Woods demands.

"What?" Lewis looks at me perplexed.

I shrug.

"You heard me, the gardener. Which one of you jerks grows the greens, man?" pushes Woods.

"Neither," I say quickly, but I guess where he's leading us.

"Sure, someone on Peter's wing is a dab-hand gardener?" He leans down and rests his bullnecked head on his palms. His fish eyes are level with ours.

Nothing scares Woods because Woods is too stupid to comprehend fear or shit about anything.

His tobacco tongue spits out the words. "I said, which one grows the greens, man?"

Now I'm certain. It's Walter. News of Walter's wacky backy magic, the Peanut Wizard, has finally made it to eager ears and they've hatched a plan to utilize the boy's talents on the inside. Only as irritating as Walter is, I'm not sending trouble his way. No way could that lump of emotional blubber handle Woods and his merry men.

"Not on our wing, man. I don't know anyone. Sure you've got the right zone?" I suggest.

Woods pins his a gaze right at mine; he waits, he measures me up. He gauges my response. Only I hold steady. I'm not shifting man, or Wally Walter's dead meat.

He knows I'm keeping it masked and he's not a happy chappy.

Woods sniggers. He stretches his stinking fingers across my face, tosses my chips on to the table and helps himself from the pile.

He chews it slowly with an inane grin and watches my blood fuel up to a sparking.

I could take him on. I could do some real damage, but I'm not an idiot; he's got a whole gang backing his big ugly ass: one maybe, twenty? No.

"I'll ask around, no worries," Lewis blurts to cut the tension. "I'll find out for you, man. It'll be a piece of piss."

I breathe out, slowly, while Lewis is holding the peace, keeping things steady.

"Sure you will. You'll bring me that name," says Woods, rising slowly.

He spits his half-chewed chip back on to my pile. "Fuck you," he hisses, as he strolls away.

I look at my chips and decide they're for the waste bucket.

That beautiful prism has disappeared from the table-top. I stare down at a heap of white spit on the melamine surface with my guts still churning.

I wonder how Mum's doing. Strange! When I'm feeling my most vulnerable, my most challenged, I think about her and Harrie and everything aches inside.

CHAPTER 4

Nights give me flashbacks or nightmares. I can't differentiate. It happens in my sleep like nightmares, but it's a recall of reality.

Weird!

I rarely revisit those days when I used to be someone else: a happy younger brother, an almost ideal son. Instead I tumble down that same dark shaft; the one that draws me through time with an agonising crash into this cold slab of a bed.

Last night, I was living at home, out on the street having fun as usual. My mates were there: Millsy, Leo, Ollie and the rest. I could hear them, "Heya, Bouncy boy, come back: fun's just started."

Only I needed some air, to get a breath before going back to the fun. There was the whole night to cruise through.

I stepped out, the cars flashed by, there was a slight drizzle in the air. It felt cool on my hot skin, refreshing. But my head was full of floating, and music and happiness.

Then, Harrie caught sight of me from across the road. She was walking with Rich, the guy who was and probably still is head-over.

His face was, as always, focused, attentive. His bright blue eyes had already developed fine laughing lines and he wore that calm expression that said, 'I'm easy with life and it's easy with me.'

He knew his own mind; he wanted to be with Harrie forever. I could tell. He was smitten and I was the genetic pull, the gel that would keep him with her.

Shit! Why did I come out of the rave? Why did we collide? What drew Rich and Harrie to my end of town? My end was full of empty shops, disused warehouses, it was a kids' paradise.

But that night, it's like the universe designed it that way; realigned those stars so we'd be magnetically drawn together at high impact. We all flew full velocity, unstoppable into a deadly explosion!

Ollie has passed me some candy. Whatever! It was potent stuff: it sent the world spiralling through a kaleidoscope. Everything looked beautiful yet strangely distorted. It was powerful, magnificent, surreal! I loved everyone and everything, man.

It was like floating in a wonderful world, trouble-free, full of positive charges. I'd staggered out of the throbbing music to meditate on the cool night air. The streets transformed into a cartoon – time flicked and flashed, flicker flicker, beep beep.

"Come on, Lawrence, you're pissing everyone off." Rich's voice echoes across the road to me.

He sounds friendly, calm, his voice singing, "Come with me, come home. Come with me, come home."

Yeah, like it's a show. It's OK, it's just Rich singing.

BALANCE

I can't believe the brief moment in time as it pans out through my shifting universe, my warping world, Harrie's taking a hand in hand walk with lover boy and finds me stoked at a rave.

Harrie's calling to him, her voice is strange, like a guitar humming in my head. "Leave it, Rich, leave it, Rich Rich Rich, yeah yeah. He's off his head again, again, again, whoo hoo."

I can see, even from a distance, her hair. It's waving on her head like Medusa's, but no snakes, just wild, crazy, bright fizzing red hair, sparks, sparks.

But Rich isn't going to leave it. Rich wants to show Harrie how much he cares about her. How much he wants to be the pseudo big brother; the one who helps me sort my stupid little life out. It's OK. He's going to have a word with me. He's going to get me right back on track. It's about authority, man, authority.

He's walking toward me across the road in that paternal 'I know what to do' way and I can see the game, level one, duck and dive the approaching bot; the computer says, "You have three lives left."

I look at the fire escape. I can get high, high, I'm higher than a kite.

But deep inside a reality tugs at the high I'm in.

"Lawrence, for Christ's sake, get your stupid ass here, now." Rich's voice is blowing across the road to me, blowing with a surge of cold reality in the night air.

Gotta get my head in gear then, no games, man, no games.

"You little shit. Come back, I just want to talk."

"Hey, Rich, stay man, come inside, man, come inside," I'm calling. "We're all good. Got friends, they're good friends."

But I feel like a stinking lowlife. I haven't been home for two days, or is it three?

"Lawrence, what the hell are you doing here? What are you playing at? My texts, you little sod, eight texts, eight. You're unbelievable." Harrie's drifting like a phantom towards me.

Rich: I can smell his aftershave and he's right on to me.

It's the guilt, man. Seeing them gives me the guilt mingled with the game, the game is on. I just need a bit more time to get my head sorted. After this night I'll get back on track. Go cold turkey. I can do it.

But not tonight.

I turn to escape: to outmanoeuvre the approaching Rich bot.

The Rich bot is already engaged.

"Hold on, you little sod," Rich is shouting. "I want a word with you, *you, you*."

Game on...

He's speeding up, hopping over the shit cans and bottles as I grab the metal rails and clamber up. He's coming.

Rich is a nice guy. Rich: a really nice guy, but he's a bot, hop, hop, bot.

I'm not such a nice guy; I'm off my little tree.

Fire escape, up, clang, clang and the Rich bot's clanging behind.

I think I might fly. I hold out my arms, yay! The world is immense, man. It's beautiful. I'm in the fresh night air, the wind slamming against my face, cooling my cheeks.

There're shadows, arms, bodies, ghosts dancing in the darkness, a pain in my mouth, pain.

Crack!

His coat, it's swooping like a kite, empty, flying in the air, up high, coat, fly, fly.

Rich was talking, then shouting, then ...

Harrie's screaming.

There's so much noise, machines, bright, flashing blue beneath the starry sky. Shouts, sirens and I'm down and – where're the stars, man? Where's the night sky? I put up my fists. Where's the Rich bot? Beep, beep.

Game over.

You have lost three lives.

I wake up and my hands are clutching the cold rim of my bed. I remember where I am. I'm banged up. I hear a shout. Shit! It's me and my voice is still reverberating around my tiny cage.

It's never dark in this place. It's never night. There's always a dull yellow light piercing through the consciousness: institution light, penetrating, searching.

I get up and switch on my main light.

They're waiting: Harrie's letters. Stacks of white envelopes all wrapped in the elastic bands I ferreted from the post room.

At my desk, I slowly pull her latest offering out of the bundle. Her handwriting's changed over the past months. I look at the first letter, drawing it tentatively from the very back of the bundle, then I raise her last and compare. There's a subtle change in the slant and line of her scrawl, but it's there.

What does that mean?

She'll be well in term at uni now: set on the path to success. I wonder which course she chose, English Lit or Law? I snigger; must be Law.

The parentals will be chuffed to bits, proud-as-punch, over-the-moon, until they think of me. Hey, it all evens out in the end: one good egg, one bad egg, that's the way the scales have tipped.

I shove the letter back on to the front of the pile. It's not happening. I'm not going to ease her conscience. It's her problem. She's the one who put me in here. She'll have to come to terms with what she's done in her own good time, if ever.

Could I have done that to her? No! The answer comes back, certain, emphatic, true. I would never have betrayed her. She was everything that was good in my life. She was on the level, protective, caring and I loved her.

Nights are long inside when you can't sleep. I could shuffle out into the viewing office and have a friendly chat with a warden, talk about why I'm not sleeping. They write it all down, I know. They pretend it's a cosy little conversation just between timers and them. They nod, make the right noises, ask the right questions, but they never give any answers. It's all, "Uh huh, I see, hummm, and why do you feel like this?"

Right! I don't think so. They put you at ease, smile, make attentive grunts as you spew your life's troubles, the confessional without the priest, man. Then as soon as you go back to your room, it's all down in black and white for the rehab and key-workers to pour over, to regurgitate at some later date, when it's convenient, when it fits their plans. File on file, tick, tick, tick. Some cosy conversation!

BALANCE

That aside, there're the psychos watching the movements of their inmates; just waiting to see who cosies up to the wardens, risky.

No, I stay put, right where I am, walking up and down and around in circles, playing music over and over again in my head and watching the sky wash over from black to silver and powder blue. Just as night lifts, my head hits the pillow and if I'm lucky, I'm out. If I'm unlucky, I'm awake and screaming inside.

But like I say, don't feel sorry for me, I don't, on the level, it's just the way it is.

"Shit! What the hell are you doing?" I snap.

It's six-fifteen in the morning and I'm gazing up into the ugly face of Walter. He's standing over me, leaning across my bed and smiling like some sick monkey.

"Sorry, Lawrence. I've brought you this." Walter's ramming a pot plant in my face. I mean a real Mother's Day, bursting with pink petals, pukey pot plant.

"Christ, is this for real?" I still can't believe the horrific apparition.

"I know, I know, it's early. It's just I've got to go to the nursery. I need to prick off the tomato plants before breakfast."

"Prick what?" I'm in Neverland: it's surreal.

"Tomatoes. Or they don't shoot right. They get too bushy, then the fruits not so..."

"Whoa, rewind, man." I'm glaring at Wally with the plant and I'm seriously irked.

"Sorry, Lawrence, but I've grown this specially for you. It's a cyclamen. I know you wake up, Lawrence, at night. I hear you sometimes pacing, shifting things around. It's bad when you can't sleep. I do the same, you know. I can't sleep. It's cabin fever, that's what it is. It gives me stomach-ache. Only I thought it would be nice for you to have something to look at when you're up in the night."

I sit up and shake my head.

"What frickin business is it of yours if I don't sleep?"

"None, I'm not saying it is. I'm just saying I understand and you've always been nice to me. Not like some of the others. You don't make me feel bad. You never make me feel bad. Anyway, I'm just giving you this to look at when you're awake," says Walter.

Walter's nervous now: jumpy, he backs off and dumps the plant on my table like a loaded weapon, next to my letter pile.

"Sorry. Didn't mean anything by it. Just water it once a week," he says, as he flees the room.

I gaze at the full blooms and groan. That kid is seriously challenged. I also realise that if I don't drag my heap of bones out of the sack now, I'll fall back to sleep and L. James will chew me to pieces.

Three hours kip, that's all I've had for the night.

I could speak to the medic and get some sleepers, though they're tough on handing those out in here. It's been known for some kids to save them up, overdose and die as a result. Now there's a surprise!

So they'd expect me to talk about my problems, try and work them through before any sleepers came my way.

Sure, let's start with, I want to beat the shit out of the old man and tell Mum I know everything, her fantasy land's been blown. Oh! And while we're on it, the only person I really trusted in my sad young life betrayed me. Rich, the guy I loved, is in pieces and I've got a criminal record.

No, talking's not going to work.

See, words change nothing and I keep coming back to Mum's favourite Lennon song. She kept those lyrics pinned to the fridge till they were covered in butter, pasta and all the shit. But now, they're clean and clear to me, something like 'where you are is where you're meant to be…'

Nice one, Mum. So now we both live in a cell, yeah?

I suck it up. It's three hours and I take the hit.

I make a special point of ignoring Walter throughout the day. Like I say, I'm not a nice person. And I don't appreciate people cruising into my personal space. I've seen him glancing in my direction when he's been flitting about. Like he wants me to give him a Chufty badge or something? I look the other way.

Walter's OK. I just don't want to encourage his sensitive side – if you get my meaning.

He's out soon. He hasn't got much longer. I feel sorry for him. He's just one big marshmallow. He'll never be rigged right for this world.

Then again, who is?

My biggest worry is who's going to be moving into his room?

It's tough getting myself through each day in here. But I'm doing everything I can to tip those scales up to the positive. I don't court trouble, so I'm choosy about who I spend my time with and where I spend it.

I wandered over to the shower complex on Frederick wing when I first arrived. Some lean guy with a ponytail down to his arse came up.

"Hey, got a nice one, wanta buy?" He's naked. He sticks his hand under his towel and I'm about to punch his lights out when he lifts a bottle of blues out.

"Tell you, my friend, this will take you on a trip out of this dump to heav-en-ly."

"Nah, you're OK, mate."

I needed a clear head. I'd just seen the kick-off between Lewis and Shave and I wasn't about to get off my head, even if I was in one deep, shitty trough. I was early in. Navigating my way through dangerous territory and I intended getting out on the other side in one physical piece, even if the emotional was smashed.

Ponytail shrugged and looked at me like I was a sad bastard.

I politely shoved past him and headed back to my room like a good little boy.

So I learnt pretty quick, any stuff anyone needed, Frederick's shower block is the place to do business. OK, so the wardens cotton on, break it up and the inmates re-establish their swapsies of pills and smokes in another place. But they always move back.

But, I can't afford it, not only money: I'm not flush in here. I don't tap my family for cash, too many issues, and I don't want to be in here any longer than the second I'm due out. But without the stuff, without the smokes and the highs and the lows — it's just one long painful existence, on the level.

There's another one. L. James dumps Harrie's next letter down on my counter.

"Someone loves you," he says with a wink.

BALANCE

I smile feebly and slip it into my pocket.

"What are you going to do when you're out, Lawrence? Have you spoken to careers yet?" He tosses a glance and a pile of browns in my direction. I stare as usual at the long scar running down the side of his neck. Where had he got that little trophy? Maybe one day, when I get the balls, I'll ask him right out.

"No, it's too far off, sir." I start weighing the first letter.

"Twelve weeks, possibly ten after all your hard work and dedication, that's not far off. That's going to happen and it'll be on you before you know it," insists L. James.

There's a small rise in my serotonin levels at that sudden realization. But after three hours sleep, it barely registers.

"Have you spoken to careers?" prompts L. James.

"Don't think they're ready either, sir." I'm weighing it all and coming up with nothing. The counters are bouncing, up, down, up, down, happy sad, happy sad.

"It's not about them, Lawrence, it's about you. You put in a request for a consultation and they're obliged to give you one and I think now's the time. Plan your out and it'll run smoothly."

I don't respond. What's there to say? I can't think about it.

I don't believe I'll do anything but breathe deeply and live in open spaces and never trust another human being in my life, ever again.

"The forces might be a good move," he prompts.

"That's for roughnecks!" I regretted that riposte as soon as it tumbled off my stupid tongue.

He smiles. "You'd be surprised. There're some pretty clever people in the forces, lad. They need to think – about themselves and those serving with them. It's down to looking after your own. Life or death, that's what's at stake, yours and theirs."

"Yes, sorry, I didn't mean ..." I don't dig out of that one, but he's not offended. I'm a lucky boy, today.

"You're clever, you'd fit in nicely. It's about references and support and I'd be happy to provide those," announces L. James.

I smile, to my amazement. But I don't respond. I can't engage. I'm just too whacked.

"Well, have a think about it, Lawrence. The offer's there," he says.

I feel like some missionary in disguise is recruiting me for the church, only it's guns, not bibles.

"Yes, thanks, sir."

I must look slightly dazed from my lack of sleep, a mass of flowers in my room and an offer of references from L. James, of all men.

I watch the scales rise slightly to the positive. Hold there, hold there.

It's been a long day. I drag my tired arse back to my wing, but there's a welcoming party at my door. It's Woods and his ugly son-of-a-bitch mate, Martin.

"Hey, where'd you get that nice little pot piece?" demands Woods. He's peering through my cabin window at the cyclamen, a glaring bloom of disgusting, unpalatable pink.

I know he's tried my door. I know it's locked.

I've got Harrie's letter in my hand; it's my prompt.

"My sister sent it. She thought my room needed brightening up."

BALANCE

Shark's not biting. He knows I'm lying.

As I move up to my door, he snatches Harrie's letter from my hand and all the tiredness, the weariness just washes away with the sudden surge of adrenalin, anger and a need to flatten the shithead.

"Give that back, Woods!"

"Ahh, isn't that nice? His sister's sent a pretty flower. Give this back or what, asshole?"

He's looking at Martin with a triumphant snigger.

"You're a low-life liar. Where'd that pot come from?" He points through my porthole, with my letter clutched in his grubby fingers.

"None of your fucking business." I'm ready to punch one of them before they both pulp me up, which I'm certain will happen. But just one punch, just to lay one on Woods' ugly, smirking face and I'd be at least satisfied, when I'm lying in that medical wing.

He steps up nose to nose and raises Harrie's letter in the air. "You want to read this? Give me a name."

"How about shithead?" I declare.

"You're dead meat," says Woods.

Those scales wobble, twelve weeks, maybe ten turn to fifteen weeks, maybe twenty, good behaviour, bad behaviour, up, down, up, down, down I go again.

The voice of reason rises above our stupid little hot heads.

"Now then, that's enough," says Warden Amy.

Amy's built like a tank and he rolls up to us on his homing device.

"What, sir?" says Woods.

"What nothing," Amy says flatly. "This isn't your patch, Woods. Why are you in this area?"

"Just paying a visit, sir," says Woods.

He retreats as Amy draws nearer and I grab my chance, snatching my letter out of his hand.

"Wanker," Woods hisses at me.

I stare back in triumph, but I'm angry, angry as shit.

"It's not free time now, Woods; no one's given you permission to be over here, have they? Have you got a slip?" Amy holds out his hand.

"Nah, sorry, sir. Couldn't find the warden to get one," says Woods.

"Well, you toddle back and get that paperwork before you come into other areas, understood? I could put you on report for this," threatens Amy.

"Ah sir, don't do that. I've not done anything," whines Woods, raising his arms.

"Me neither, sir," pipes up Martin, shaking his head like a wobble dog. "Not guilty."

"Don't get mouthy with me, son," snarls Amy. His eyes darken as he glares at the two cocky inmates tossing words back at him and I see he's tensed up and ready to go on the attack.

"No sir, sorry. Won't happen again," whines Martin. He's giving Amy a pathetic attempt at an affable smile, but it looks like he's going to puke.

"Piss off back to your house and get the proper permission, you two. Go on, scram," snaps Amy.

Woods skulks away with Martin on his tail.

"Trouble?" Amy asks, when Woods and Martin are safely dispatched through the door.

"No, no trouble. He just wanted to ask about the post room." Amy knows I'm lying too. But I don't give a toss.

What scares me more than Woods, Martin, L. James or Amy for that matter is the sudden realisation that I would have tipped those scales way over to the negative and flattened Woods, if Amy hadn't turned up.

No out in ten weeks. No escape from the four walls I've stared at for nearly three years. No freedom to walk out of a door whenever to wherever. I could have put another three months on my time here.

What a sad, stupid bastard I am.

CHAPTER 5

In the education complex sunshine beats warmth onto my head through the skylights.

I'll tell Lewis we must live in an attic with skylights.

They're glorious: like you can see heaven rolling past, giving a glimpse of somewhere beyond those big white puffy clouds. And there's a whole world out there: our earth spinning in space, in a universe full of life, gravitation holding it all together, existence in a blink. Yeah, it's immense, awesome through that window.

Her voice filters through and my neck's aching like hell. How long have I been staring up? Who knows? But I'm back in the education complex and it's cool here.

I did a spell in the art classes and did some good work, even if I say so myself. OK, I'm no Hockney or Blake, but at least I tried. They shipped this local artist guy in on a special arts programme. He was all denim and sandals, intense and dramatic, but the weirdo got us producing some decent stuff. Our work was going to be displayed in the local library and we were going to get a day out to see the event, until some kid with issues had a problem with my picture and thought he'd literally piss on it.

BALANCE

My watercolour ran all right, right down the easel and on to the floor. Although, on an artistic visual front, OK, I admit, it improved the overall effect of the piece, like impressionist, a pissed-on bouquet. But it was a no-goer; it stank of pee.

So now, I'm doing English Lit and when I glance up at the roof-light, that child in me wants to be an astronaut. I had dreams. I think of Harrie and our plans for uni and after, all those things we talked about. Before she got the hots for Rich, we said we'd take a year, travel. I sat up late one night with Harrie with a map of the world. We'd highlighted the H & L trail of all the places we planned to take in.

A paper jabs my eye and jolts me to the now. I look round but no-one's giving it away.

I've ploughed through *Enduring Love*. Now I have to write something interesting about it. All I can think is that Jed Perry's seriously out to lunch and Joe has got a real problem he needs to deal with.

Somehow, I see the book can be real. It all works and I can imagine life being like that. Some weird event happening that changes people's lives forever: all in one deep breath.

I take that deep breath in.

Then I think, yes, that's how it happens, quick as a frickin flash.

"But the language, just think, are there biblical aspects to this story? What is the writer doing?" asks Miss Hayden, our English tutor.

My hand goes up. Why the hell did I do that? But I've got something to say for a change and it's on its way out and I can't plug it.

"It's about fate: like, invisible forces drawing the characters together. A collision of lives exploding, bang! Then the shock waves rolling out to all those other characters you don't see, they're out of sight, but they're impacted and they're a part of what's driving the story."

There's silence as Miss Hayden moves up a step to listen in, to see the weirdo who's talking, so I run with it.

"Biblical, Miss? The balloon rising up and inside's this kid rising higher, closer to death. Instant, those seconds are decision time. The kid needs the ultimate sacrifice of a life. Salvation? Biblical? Like the Crucifixion. No, no way. There was no preordained path. It's about which action they took. If they'd turned away, they'd be different people, without compassion, humanity. The story? Live as one person, or die as another. It's all about weighing it up, balancing it out."

There're rows of heads all straining round and staring at me and Miss Hayden's fronting them up, looking completely fazed. She's poised, mouth open, but nothing's coming out.

Then she smiles, self-consciously, and looks kind of pleased.

Either she's not used to me responding, or she hasn't got a shitting clue what I'm talking about.

But she's polite and patient. "Yes, that's an interesting and thought-provoking evaluation, uh, Lawrence," she says tentatively, "so let's meditate further on this and you can write it up. It's good to put your thoughts down on paper."

That's Miss Hayden's way of saying you talk drivel so I start to scribble the drivel.

And while I write, I begin to wonder what the hell I am going to do on release from this place? L. James tossed me a loaded question.

I know I don't ever want to come back. But it's not about the negatives, is it! I can say what I don't want for the rest of my sad little life.

Problem is, what I do want isn't tangible, visible. The truth.

So how does that answer L. James' question? Maybe I should pick up a gun, put on the khakis and join his merry men. Shit, no!

One thing's for sure, I don't want English Lit.

CHAPTER 6

"Visitor, Lawrence." Warden Amy's tapping on my open door.

"Who is it, sir?" I need to know if it's Harrie, although she hasn't tried to visit since my transport here. She tried to see me four, maybe five times when I first arrived and I made sure she failed.

"Mr Gregory, from services," says Amy. "Come on, chop-chop, he's a busy man."

We're out of Peters' wing and some warden I don't recognize takes custody of me from Amy. He strides me across the outside green to the main offices.

I haven't been here before: it's new, different. I suddenly realise there are other places, buildings, shapes and existences outside of my room on the wing.

I wonder who Gregory is. Maybe he's education or employment. I begin to lighten my step. I'm actually talking about this now, the out. I'm thinking about a future, man. But I hold myself back. I can't let my emotions run free; too much feeling in here and you're done.

I'm escorted down a light, airy corridor. There are people at desks inputting on PCs, talking on the phone, tapping keyboards, hammering buttons on vending machines: ordinary life.

The warden stops and puts his arm up to block my advance, then he knocks on the door.

I stand and wait like a schoolkid ready to go in to see the head.

"Come in," a voice instructs.

The warden opens the door and ushers me forward.

Some middle-aged guy is sitting with a load of files spread across a coffee table.

It's like I've stepped into someone's living room: low leather sofas, a vase of flowers on the window, magazines under the coffee table, pictures on the walls and designer lamps. It's all pale blues and soft greens on the carpet.

He stands and reaches out to shake my hand.

"Lawrence, hello, I'm Mr Gregory. Good to see you." He says it like I'm someone special.

I shake his hand and hover. I feel like I've walked into a parallel universe. You know, the nice Lawrence, the successful Lawrence, the Lawrence who deserves respect.

Then I glance down at HMYOI Hendbrook stamped across the yellow file and I get a punch in the emotional gut. Yeah, welcome back, loser.

Gregory looks friendly, easy-going. He's greying at the sides, his face is creased into comfortable lines drawing out from his fine, silver specs. He's relaxed.

He indicates to a low leather seat across the table.

"Plonk yourself down there, why don't you?" he says.

Yes! Why don't I? I wonder what he wants from me. My senses pick up a want, a need, a requirement.

He shuffles his papers and shoves them neatly back into a folder on the table.

Nice as he is, he's official all right.

"I suppose you're wondering why I've come to see you, Lawrence," he says.

I nod. "I thought maybe careers."

"Almost, not quite. It's a stepping-stone to thinking about careers, your future. It's all a part of the rehabilitation," he says, nodding and giving a reassuring smile.

"OK?" I'm looking around, soaking up the new environment. My mind's tossing the word rehab around in circles, up and down. It's not comfortable or uncomfortable. Stay cool, it's just a word.

"I'm part of the SORI project," he says. "Ever heard of that?"

My heart sinks like a hammer in the gut. Thump! A sickening surge of anger bubbles to the surface.

I've been duped.

"Yes, it's where the victims torment the criminals, a kind of getting your own back," I state.

He smiles and frowns all in one.

"That's the view of people who've never been involved in the project. You'd get a completely different take on it if you spoke to the parties who've engaged in this process."

My pea brain is suddenly grasping the fact that this guy wants me to face Rich. He literally wants me to see Harrie's boyfriend, or ex. I never angled to see how all that panned out, too harrowing.

I was just told Rich'd live; thank Christ! And that was the end of it.

BALANCE

But this guy wants me to relive the horrors of that night, to confront the broken, disfigured face of Rich and he thinks I'll be OK with it?

The thought fills me with revulsion. Waves of panic flood over me. I start coughing, like I'm choking as every sinew in my body contracts.

"I can't see him. I'm sorry. I mean genuinely sorry. On the level. I never intended for him to be hurt so badly. But no way." I jabber on as I slowly rise from my seat, hoping he's not seen me prep for an escape.

"It's not just about you, though, is it, Lawrence? Have you not considered that perhaps Richard Groves wants to move on with his life too? This would help him." Gregory's voice is determined.

My hands are sweating, my fingernails gouge into my palms. I stand, paralysed: trapped in a room of unfolding terrors, pictures colliding in my head with the sickening wash of colour around me.

I suddenly long for the safety of my cell, for the whitewashed brick, keeping me in, and everything painful, challenging out.

I feel the weight; it's pushing me down. I need to resist; I need to push back. I'm biting my lip and staring out of the window for an exit.

"You don't have to meet him. That's true," continues Gregory, "And all things considered, it could cut a few weeks off your term. But that's not the point, is it, Lawrence? I'm here to help you and Richard Groves. No hidden agenda. It's just about people moving on. Giving every person involved the best chance for a new future. This programme is designed to do just that, criminal and victim," he says, looking up at me.

He sits waiting in silence and assessing my response.

Then he leans back in the chair, relaxed, cheerful. But really shitting relaxed, like there's no panic, no problem.

Right? There is a big shitting problem.

"I can hang on for three more weeks," I state, categorically.

He puts his hand up and slowly rubs his chin, contemplating.

"You look like a bright lad to me..."

I roll my eyes; here we go with the pep talk.

"I'm sure you can hang on for three weeks. What's three weeks after three years?"

"Exactly!" At last, the guy's getting the point.

"But it's not about three weeks in here, is it, Lawrence? It's about the rest of your life out there. Supposing you meet Richard on the street or on a bus? That would be a matter of luck for you both. You'd have the opportunity to talk: get things out into the open. But what are you going to say to him? Sorry? You and I know that this needs more than that. I think you have the intelligence to work this out."

He pauses while he watches me swallow back and choke on his words. Then he goes for it.

"The wardens say a lot of good things about you. They get to know their charges over their term here. They wouldn't put you up for this if they didn't think you couldn't handle it."

He slides an envelope across the coffee table and taps it with his finger before withdrawing.

I stare down at it, my hand hovering as if poised over an unexploded bomb.

"It's my job to make sure it all works out as best it can on this one," he says. "No need to decide now."

He indicates for me to take the letter. His gaze is insistent, confident.

"Is this from my sister?" I ask, but I check the handwriting: it's not hers.

"What?" he asks, glancing up in confusion.

"Nothing, nothing. OK. Can I go now?"

He stands and reaches to shake my hand.

"Just pop your head in the office next door. The warden will escort you back. Oh, and thank you for considering this."

He smiles like I'm his friend and I almost feel like I am until he indicates to the envelope, ensuring I take possession of it before I leave the room.

I hover, then I snatch it up and I'm out of that door.

CHAPTER 7

I'd shoved the letter into my back pocket and it stayed there, stressing the shit out of me all week. I kept putting my hand in and out to check it was there and hoping it wasn't.

I almost lost it to the voluptuous Officer Pevensey, in the roughs I'd dumped into my laundry tote. I managed to rifle through the wing's stinking tubs; courage, man, that's what I had. I needed to retrieve that envelope before it went for the wash.

"You boys! What's so important you need to dig down through that crap? You'll catch all sorts in there, Heathcliff, but not what you're hoping for, sweetie," joked Pevensey, as I tossed out filthy, skid-stained boxers and slimy socks.

She suspected I had some skunk or pills stashed away. No such thing.

And when I pulled out the letter, her brows almost touched the tip of her badly cut fringe.

"Voila!" I cried, lifting the envelope into the air and kissing its creased seal. "Today an envelope, tomorrow a rabbit, mon ami."

She laughed like a kid and to my surprise I laughed with her.

BALANCE

Thank Christ: my dreams of Officer Pevensey and her sultry dances have stopped. I was about to book myself into the psycho wing.

Problem is, they've been replaced with less savoury images, if that's possible. Flashbacks, cries of agony, trigger jolts of despair in the night.

I wonder, maybe I should read it, this letter. Maybe I should tear the seal and look inside: anything to stop the night terrors.

They're getting worse. I'm waking up three, maybe four times a night. I'm wondering if it's because I'm close to the out?

Last night, I woke in a bed of sweat. I rolled out and stumbled to the hatch in my door.

I was ready to beat at the bars, hammer on the metal. My fists hit the cold, but I stopped short. I was going to call for Amy. I wanted out. I wanted the pills to take away the shakes, the nausea, the past.

I'm so close to freedom and I'm tilting at windmills, man.

I'M ANGRY AND SCARED LIKE A BABY.

CHAPTER 8

Over the past few days Walter's been acting weird. An odd statement, I accept, as the definition of Walter is 'weird'.

But he's been strangely quiet, reserved, even sombre. Walter's never been serious in that grown-up, meditative kind of way before. He slinks into the canteen, eats, then disappears. He pads down the corridors, morose, pensive, like he's figuring out the meaning of life and death.

I've always thought of Walter as a bit of a cartoon. He hops down the corridor like a turkey on a pogo stick and always sports an inane grin, like he wants to be happy and everyone's friend.

That's what's been so irritating about Walter and yet that's what's starting to concern me, his absence of Walterness.

I've been battling with my conscience, asking myself should I talk to him, should I prise the problem out of him in a sort of distant, cool, disinterested kind of way?

When he's been shuffling past in the mornings, there's no whistles, no glancing in to see if he can pin me down for a lesson on the composites of friggin compost. No, he's just head down, silent.

BALANCE

But then, if I prod him to come clean, would that mean he'd continue to irritate the shit out of me and the rest of the idiots on Peters' wing? Do I want the jerk cosying up to me and shadowing me like always?

My internal battle lasted a mere three seconds.

The 'No' vote won. I concluded, he can talk to the wardens; that's what they're paid to do, listen.

Bet they get a hefty bonus for the service too, after gaining all those extra certs in psychotherapy on away weekends at some hotel, chewing over the challenges of dealing with young offenders before meeting at the bar for a jolly.

I'd like to pick one of those psychology experts up and dump him or her in the middle of Lewis' estate for a year to deal with the drugs, knives and domestic violence.

Wonder how they'd talk themselves out of that unsavoury little situation? Yeah! Not so shitting jolly.

Still, I guess some people have to talk their way through some problems or life would get pretty messy.

Talk of the devil! Fate is like that; I'm musing over some question and life throws it right back in my face for good measure.

"Can I talk?" Walter's hovering in my doorway looking pathetic.

He's been blubbing. His eyes are red and puffier than usual. His spiky hair's sticking out at all angles under his beanie and he's reminding me of some kid from a bad sitcom.

"What now, Walter? I'm kind of busy."

Hey, like I said, I'm not a nice person.

"It's urgent; it's life or death," he says. "Please, please, Lawrence, I'm in a real fix."

It's not the please, please, that does it: it's the genuine look of terror in the guy's eyes.

I can't back off now. I've got nowhere to go. Like I'm stuck in this room, no back door and he's dug in here right in my friggin doorway.

"Yes, OK, but, hold on, don't close the door, Walter, don't want rum ..."

But Walter's already clicked the lock and we're trapped in Agony Aunt land.

I note that move was uncharacteristically aggressive of him.

"I'm not any good at this, Walter. I need you to know that. I mean, like there are trained people out there who can get you sorted a lot quicker than I can, mate."

He's not taking the pitch.

"If I go to the wardens, they'll cut me. They've told me, they'll cut me to pieces." Walter's shaking now, shaking badly.

I sit up straight at my desk, almost knocking over his plant pot. It is serious.

"OK, sit down, man. It's OK," I say quickly.

Something has stirred him to a mush and he needs help.

"I'm in trouble, Lawrence. They're out to hurt me if I don't do like they say," he whimpers.

"Stay cool, Walter. There're things you can do. We can get you moved to another wing." I try to sound confident, calm.

"They're in all the areas, man. I know. There's a ring of them. They're a nethreerk. Like the freakin Mafia. They're machines," he says.

And what scares me is – he's right. Once you're a target it's tough getting out of their sights.

He rubs the tears away with the back of his grubby sleeve.

"What are they after?" I ask, but I'm pretty clear I already know.

"Plants. They've got them and they need me to cultivate somewhere hidden. They've got it all figured out ..."

He gazes out of my porthole. "I've only got a short while left, Lawrence. I told them that. I said, it's not worth it and if I get caught, if I get caught, that's what I'm in for. I'll get hammered down for years. I'll never get out, never. But they don't give a shit. They just don't care, they don't."

His whole body is juddering and I'm lost on what to do. I can't figure how I can help him.

I genuinely feel pretty shitty for the guy.

One thing I do know is that the ring is made of animals. I've heard bad things, seen people get sliced up and burnt.

The ring's a nethreerk of feral kids. Their only loyalty is to their tribe, the crew. All of them are on fixed careers to their next prison, it's set in stone and they'll wear their sentences like badges of honour.

But not Walter, Walter's just a sad, lonely kid.

"What are you going to do, Walter? What's the plan? Maybe it's worth pitching for a transfer, a few weeks somewhere else then you're home free," I suggest, feeling a tad selfish at the thought of shifting the problem.

But he's locked in. He's too scared to move; he's trapped in his own skin, squirming on the seat and wishing he was someone else.

"I want you to talk to them; tell them I'm due release, tell them I can't give them what they want. Tell them to find someone else – just," he implores and I whistle an objection.

I look at him dumbfounded, like he's crazy!

"Shit, Walter. What's the point of me taking them on? They'll pulp me. There's no way they're going to listen to me, no way." I raise my hands, "Sorry, Walter, but it's a bad idea and I'm not up for it."

It's a no-goer.

My sense of self-preservation kicked in the day I was escorted through those gates. Now that I was so close to walking back out in one piece, I intended to keep it that way.

"But if you don't, I don't know what they'll do, Lawrence. I'm in a tight hole, man. I know they'll listen to you, I know they will. That Woods and the others, they respect you. They know you're sound."

He breaks into sobs and I turn and gaze vacantly at the poster on my wall; it's my escape. It's a picture of a cityscape for the latest movie they're showing in the rec room. I took it. I rolled it up and shoved it in my pocket because it's somewhere that's nowhere. I can imagine I am there, in this perfect place full of my old friends and freedom.

I look back at Walter. It's sad to see him running scared, but I know where I stand and I'm not shifting; this is the way it is.

"Lawrence, you can handle them, I can't," he insists between sniffs.

"You're crazy, Walter. I can't cure this for you. You've got to speak to the wardens. They'll give you protection until you leave. It's a no-brainer."

BALANCE

He coughs and splutters, then quietens down as I shift uncomfortably in the small space.

"I thought you'd help," he says quietly and it cuts me up for him to see me as the disappointment I am. It's a perspective I've grown accustomed to.

"Hey, listen, Walter. It's your call. But I'd pitch at your key-worker, for Christ's sake. Come on, man. You can sort this. You've got the balls to do it."

Walter's rubbing his mucky hands down his trouser legs, reflective, silent, lost. He stays and just stares out of my cell window for what seems like a lifetime, then looks up at me and gives a pathetic weird smile.

"How's the plant doing?" Walter's looking at the pink wilting petals and I'm feeling guilty at not watering it for a few days.

It's a twisted train of thought, but I can see he's gone in his head: Walter's someplace else, now.

I turn and wince at the pinkish grey sea of blooms.

"Yeah, I'm working at keeping it alive. I water it just like you say. OK, sometimes, if it's an early one with L. James, maybe not. But mostly it's job done."

I smile, but there's a silent acknowledgement, a shift in our relationship, a change in the balance.

He stands up slowly and sighs deeply.

Then he shrugs. "Keep watering," he says, soberly.

"Sure." I nod and ask, "You going to be OK? Are you going to have a chat with Amy or L. James? He's definitely your guy. Or I could talk to the wardens for you."

I hear the words trip off my tongue and wonder where the hell they've come from, but something in that sentiment causes a brief flash of emotion and recognition in Walter's eyes.

"No, it's good, Lawrence. I think I can keep my head down, keep out of their way for a few frickin weeks. For Christ's sake," he exclaims, like it's one big joke.

I nod: but we both know that's a no-hoper.

"Thanks for listening, Lawrence," he says quietly.

Then he's gone.

I lean on my desk and sink my head into my hands. I feel like a heel.

At lunch, Lewis makes me feel a whole lot better.

"You'd be off your trolley, man, to get mixed up in that shit. Walter needs to fight his own battles or he'll stay a baby for the rest of his life. If he doesn't start fighting, he'll end up being everybody's bitch. He sure is pathetic," declares Lewis.

"Back off! He's not pathetic, Lewis. Come on, what's the problem with being kind these days? Who turned being nice into being a sad bastard?" I snap.

But the guilt is eating me up.

"Hey, cool down. I know he's harmless, man. But maybe he needs to be less nice and toughen up, arse face. Look, nobody does anyone any favours by fighting their battles. I know. I've grown up having to win my own and that's with two older brothers causing shit around me. You get mixed up, you get done over: that's the game. What's the point? He'll be OK. He'll work it out no pro," says Lewis.

I convince myself he's right, but there's a nagging anxiety chewing at my core and I know it's not going to go away.

Penny, our warden, wanders over. She's been recruiting in the dining hall. I've been watching to see, no takers.

"Lads, we're a few short for the rugby this week, how about pitching in?" she demands.

"What's happened to the last ones? They in the morgue, miss?" asks Lewis.

"You're a bright spark, Lewis. Come on, the fresh air and exercise'll do you good."

"Thing about rugby is, it's not footie. See, if it was footie, I'd have a go. But rugby? Now that's a different ball game," says Lewis.

"Lawrence? What do you say?" says Penny.

"Definitely a different ball game, miss. Rugby you can hold the ball, footie, you..."

"All right, smart arses. Well, if you change your mind there's an away match at the Cheshires," she offers as she moves on to her next victims.

I'm watching for Walter. I wonder where he is, what's going on and I don't like the feeling. I shove my food in like I'm on a timer.

"You want to take over my job in the post room when I go?" I ask, because I know it's a good call. L. James is a real heavyweight on the positive of those scales.

"Are you kidding? Commander James, that freakin lunatic puts the shits up me," exclaims Lewis, "like the guy's a machine. Have you seen the scar down his face? I reckon it runs past his arse. Yeah, in fact, it might be the end of his arse. I'd rather help the harpy in the laundry room – at least she's got boobs."

I laugh.

That's how it is inside, negative to positive, swinging those scales.

CHAPTER 9

It happened at three in the morning.

I heard a scream. It cut through the wall of deep sleep into my consciousness, making my body twist and roll and I opened my eyes in panic to gaze up at the dim circular light hanging over my head, the cold eye of the watchman.

At first, I thought it was Walter. I thought they were in there, cutting him up. I thought I was listening to the horrors of my own rejection.

It was Harrie's scream.

I realised that once I'd fully come round. I hear it every night now; the same pitch, piercing through my body, filling every vein, artery with ice-cold terror.

It never changes, the sickening horror of that sound rolling back from the depths of my memory to punish me even more than being shut in my cell.

I put my light on. I need to do this to see the furniture, the walls, the shit room I inhabit: to touch harsh reality once more.

It's OK. I acknowledge the fact that I'm still here, still paying my dues, and so I should be, right?

My hands are cold, clammy. I unroll the fists I'd been clenching through the night and feel the pain running up my wrist and into my knotted forearms.

I go to my desk and pick up Gregory's letter. I toss it from hand to hand, weighing it up like I can feel the magnitude of what's written inside on every page.

My hand's shaking as I flick it over and tear the seal, everything on automatic, not wanting to, yet it's happening, it's carrying me with it as fast as my heart's pounding.

It's open and I unfurl the A4 page.

There's a lot of ink, a lot of messy scrawl: like a kid or a drunk has written it.

I'm surprised. I skip the text, turn the page and scan down to the signature.

So, that's where I stand,
Richard

It's the middle of the night and I'm here, walking up and down, round and round. Only this time I'm clutching his letter so tightly it's getting damp in my clammy hand.

I need out. I need out of this night, out of this place, out of my head.

If only I had some smoke or a pill, I could handle it then.

It's like my body's in cold turkey, all shivers and nausea. I take some deep breaths. I go down on my haunches, balance, then rise slowly with the breath, slowing it, moving the knotted muscles.

Then, I gravitate towards the bed and sit down.

I read. My eyes move slowly across the page trying to decipher the scribble.

I've been having trouble sleeping, Lawrence. It's not just the pain in my leg, that's enough in itself. Sometimes I wonder if it was worth them saving it, for what's the benefit of a lump of useless flesh? But I've got plenty of other reasons not to sleep too. My stomach's patched up; it doesn't function like it used to, doesn't process the food. I have to fill my gut with chemicals to get it to work and the chemicals keep me awake, so they give me sleeping pills and they cause crushing headaches through the day... So I take more chemicals to combat the headaches and they twist my gut up and that adds another layer to the mess, and well, you get the point, it just goes on. You see, I'm full of metal. You know: the kind of nuts and bolts that hold the parts of a machine together so that the mechanisms function. But I'm not a machine. I'm a human being and I'm not working; not any part of me is functioning as it once used to. Truth is, I'm shot to pieces.

This isn't to make you feel worse than you already probably do. At least I pray with all my being that you feel devastated, Lawrence. I need to know that you are disgusted with yourself and that at this moment in time you are sad, unhappy, regretful.

Sounds vicious. It's not. Although I would have a God-given right to be vicious and there were many nights when I was struggling not to want you dead. That is a truth!

I would have a right to hate your guts for the rest of my shattered existence. But simply, if you weren't in that emotional place right now, if you weren't suffering – then you'd have a long way to go before you come out of this nightmare and become a decent human being: before you truly find happiness again, if ever!

BALANCE

We're just taking a different route.

We're locked in; me, you and, I know, Harrie, too. I haven't seen her since she took off to uni. She didn't abandon me. She'd never do that, not Harrie. Harrie's an angel.

I feel waves of panic and grief wash over me. The grief of losing the Rich I knew before it all happened, before that night.

I put the letter on the bed and grab the metal rail. My jaw locks, my neck feels the weight of my head, pounding, as I begin to writhe inside the confines of my own skin. So much pain flooding to the surface from the core of my being that I brace myself, while the other part of me is gripping that bed rail, forcing me to take control again; to raise the paper and continue to read.

You see, Lawrence, Harrie tore herself to pieces about both of us. She cracked up, shattered like one of those beautiful china dolls. I watched her fall apart the day you went down. She tried to hide it, to be the strong girlfriend, the valiant lover, the carer. But I knew she was with me because she felt she had to be. It's tough when love turns to obligation. She would have stayed by my side because of you. I was the debt you left behind. It wouldn't have worked. I had to let her go. And that tore me up too.

But, she was not going to have her life destroyed by what happened. So much collateral damage: it was enough that she lost the two men she loved, and the most painful for her – was losing you, Lawrence, I always knew that. She worshipped you.

Three people all in one place at one time. The chemistry set off one hell of a bomb, didn't it! It's changed our futures for good. Mine's a very different path from the one I had planned. Career's shot to hell; can't concentrate on teaching or on anything for more than an hour at a time, now. The doctor says it will improve over the next few years. What's a few years, Lawrence? What's a few years?

So, let's get to the point. It's taken every ounce of emotional strength to write this. I need you to do something for me. And I need to see you face to face, look into your eyes and hear your voice when, if, you make that pledge. Then I'll know I can move on to coping with what's left of my life. You can say 'no', turn your back and try to move on. But if I can't, then ask yourself this, Lawrence. Why the hell should you? So that's where I stand,

Richard

CHAPTER 10

"Come on, Lawrence, you're in world of your own, lad," snaps L. James as another pile of browns hits the floor by my feet.

"Shit, sorry, sir!" I scramble and snatch them up in a messy pile.

"Problems?" he says.

"No, just daydreaming," I lie.

He snorts and throws another bunch across.

"Well, that's what being in here is all about, Lawrence. Sorting out those pesky problems you're 'daydreaming' about and keeping your eye on the ball while you're doing it. Christ! It's a baby's job this, you can multi-task," he says, flicking through his list and pinning it to the board.

"Sure, sir. I'm on to it."

"Good," he says, with an authoritative grin.

I'm weighing it all up in my mind. Another letter tips the balance, another weight evens the scales.

So Rich's letter is gnawing at my gut. It wasn't what I'd expected, although I couldn't say for sure what I did expect. That's me all over, a vacuous, empty-headed jerk.

At the moment, I don't feel like I know anything about anything. I'm squeezed in a box, suffocating as the lid comes down.

Walter's frozen me out; he's floating around under some dark, foreboding cloud, like the axe is about to friggin fall. That kind of pisses me off more than the absurd clown smile he used to display.

And now all this trouble with conciliation services is mashing my brain. I wander to one place and find myself in another, the rec room, instead of the showers, the kitchens instead of the library. I'm seriously losing the plot. I'm not clever enough to figure all this out. As in English aren't As in life, they're just letters of the frickin alphabet.

That, or the fact that I hear pipe music floating out of the library and when I peer through the porthole, the Latvian's doing some weird dancing. He's all tantric, waving his arms and gyrating mahusive ugly hips. Amar's sitting behind the Vian, trying to read and when he sees me peering in he mouths some abuse behind Vian's back and gives the crazy sign.

I shrug at him in sympathy. Stuff of nightmares.

Now I'm off duty and for the first time since they slammed the door in my face, I plan to get off my head.

I found a smoke. In Frederick showers, this big Irish guy, Oscar or Oliver or what the hell does it matter?

I'd just been paid my extra for the postal services. Maybe that's what I'll be when I leave here, a jolly postman, a hearty soul, a rock of the local community in my little red fun-around. Yeah, the image brings a smirk to my face.

Anyway, I don't give jack shit! I purchased some good strong green. Just got to be careful when I'm out of control, when I'm floating.

I need to drift through all these problems until they're sorted.

Time, I've got plenty of time. But I'm not a shitting magician. I'm a teenage convict and I need the smoke to let it all fade away.

That's how I got in here, man, it all started with a smoke.

Lewis puts a smile on my face.

"No kidding, the Vian?" he exclaims. "Man, he'd friggin destroy the music." He throws his head back and laughs. "Why the shit didn't they get him on the basketball team? Gorilla'd just drop it in, we'd be top of the league. Yeah, he could dance and do the drop all in one."

"A smoke," he says gratefully, as I pass him the spliff. He inhales deeply and smiles.

This is why I hang around with Lewis; he doesn't take everything so seriously, so personally, but he doesn't take the piss either. Christ! He just gets on with life, ugly or not.

We're reclining in the corner of the football court out of sight under the lens and watching Peters' wing getting hammered by Stanton wing.

Someone's just laid a right hook on our number eleven; he's bleeding all the way down to his toes, but he's not fussed.

The whistle goes and they're off again and it's all colours floating past my eyes, the reds and the yellows and I can hear Lewis' voice in the distance saying, "Go for it, man. You've got nothing to lose. Meet the guy. I 'spose you owe him that."

I'm feeling contented. I'm feeling carefree. I say, "You're a clever dick, Lewis."

He's beaming. "Yeah, true words."

I laugh, as the reality glides through my consciousness, but gently, softly; I've given him three years of my young life, I've got a criminal record, a shattered family and shit prospects and I'll meet him, why not? I'm feeling good; I'll go for it. I'll just let the wardens know. That Gregory guy can get his fix. I can do this, I can just cruise, man, sail the rest of my life away.

CHAPTER 11

"Visitor, Lawrence." Amy taps on the door with a big smile. He's got another gold stud ear piercing, I note.

Small changes in this place are what you hang on to and it kind of adds to his hip, 'in with the kids,' iron-man image.

"Your folks are here," he says standing in the doorway looking out and monitoring activities down the hall.

"Which ones?" I ask. It could be her; it could be Harrie.

"How many parents have you got? No, don't answer – loaded question in here."

That's OK. It's not Harrie. I'm going for it.

There's something open about the place today. Maybe it's the sunshine, maybe it's the smell of cakes baking in the canteen kitchens, but there's definitely a good vibe.

I'm feeling more positive as I go down towards the rec room and the visitors' lounge.

This time, I'm not going to row with the old man. But that's for Mum's benefit, not his. I'm going to stay chilled, easy and enjoy the visit. Maybe I'm a lucky boy.

Lewis spends day after day without seeing his folks. There're no letters, no cards for him even at Christmas. There's no communication; it's as if he's been dumped on an island and left to swim his way back to Christ knows what. And I reckon he'll do it, swim all the way to shore. He's solid, real, is Lewis and what gets me is, he understands. He says, they're not savage; they can't cope. He's a smart boy.

So I guess I can take the old man's hassle just to connect with the past. I see in Mum's face she'll never stop loving me and that means something.

Harrie, she was my anchor. That night we'd sat in her room and I told her about the note I'd found and how Dad was going to punch my lights out, she'd just smiled, like she knew and everything was going to be OK.

She'd been straightening her hair. This week it was purple, like every friggin week she changed the colour. She was getting ready to take off with her latest and she looked at me and said, "Don't worry, bro. It's all good. We'll sort it together."

I never felt alone, never.

I'm thrown off course as I enter the visitors' lounge. I have one visitor. It's Mum. First ever, she's turned up on her own. Come to think of it, the folks don't generally visit on a Friday; it's always been at the weekend.

I imagine their visits must be like the outings they used to take when they went to church. Dad probably bundles her into the car, she checks her handbag for no reason, they sit in silence, then they're off, silently tootling down the road, soaking up the scenery and hating each other's guts all the way to visiting Yours Truly.

They must also hate drawing up to the institution gates, booking in through security and confirming the painful fact that their son resides in this institution rather than one of repute, the university they'd hoped I'd attend. Yes, that must wound.

But she's there, sitting at a seat by the window and smiling at me like I'm filling her with pride.

I'm warming inside; her smile can be the most uplifting thing in the world; there's no challenge, no recrimination, just me.

She stands and we embrace: a long, loving hug.

Soft – but today I don't care what anyone thinks and when I glance at the others, nobody else gives a toss either. They're all sitting, some holding hands, others talking with their guests.

That's the sign on the visitors' lounge doors: GUESTS ONLY. The lounge is off bounds at all other times, despite the fact that in the corner hangs the biggest screen in the whole complex. It's designed to tempt the inhabitants with immeasurable pleasure. It remains unplugged, a black matt screen, permanently dead, to remind us we're not party to such luxury; it's for guests. Only the guests have come to visit us, not watch TV.

"Lawrence," she says, playfully ruffling my hair.

"Stop it, Mum, you're destroying my street cred." I'm feeling whimsical as I push my hair back and flatten it down.

She smiles and taps my arm.

The room is bright, the sun is heating the shatterproof glass and it's radiating on to our cheeks and shoulders.

"No Dad today?"

"He's tied up with work at the moment, son. Not that he doesn't want to see you."

I resist a smirk at that lie.

"Anyway, rather than wait until next weekend, I decided to come on my own," she says. "Harrie went on the internet with me and we found out all the timetables. The trains run quite frequently; I was surprised. And there's a special shuttle bus." She's looking triumphant.

That's what Mum does, throws Harrie in on the periphery, just to let me know I still have a sister.

Right!

Great sorting out the bus timetable for someone you've sent down. Thanks, Harrie.

"Yeah? Hey, that's efficient," I say.

"Only once a month. They do it every last weekend of the month, so it worked out just right," she says.

A brief cloud and it passes.

"Your dad couldn't come as he's running the marathon next Sunday. You know. The one he's been practising for."

I think about him and I feel a knot in my gut: that anger again.

He's whooping it up with some skirt from the office, that's the old man marathon, pumping his ego.

But I loosen up. Today is me and Mum, now there's a bonus! That's never happened before: it's different, special.

"Right, so how often's Marathon Man been running then and why haven't you been doing it too?"

She smiles wistfully. "Every evening he runs until about nine, sometimes 'till eleven at the floodlit sports field."

"Good on him, Mum."

"Yes, him," Mum says. She glances out of the window like she doesn't want her eyes to connect with mine and that's when I'm pretty sure she knows and...

Then she's back on track with a smile. "No, Lawrence! Of course I'm not going to run. I used to row, though. Back in the day when I was at college I was in a crew. I love the water, it's such fun."

"Rowing? No kidding! Like, I knew you had a thing about water, but you, a rower?"

I lean over the table, reach out and squeeze her arm. "Where's your biceps then?"

She laughs and sits up.

"You listen, I was on the first team. Won some cups, we did."

She sits back and looks across and, for the first time in years, I see her eyes brighten with a flash of pale blue. "There're a lot of things you don't know about me and that's how it should be."

"Right, just don't put it on the net before you tell me," I say.

Then, I'm holding the thought, wondering, should I tell her now, should I say? It's OK, Mum, we all know how things are with you and the old man, so go. Me and Harrie don't need you at home any more. You're free.

But she's happy, she's here for me and I know I need to wait for the right time.

She reaches over and clutches my hand. "It's not about me, Lawrence. It never has been. It's about you. That's why I'm here."

Her eyes darken and she looks at me, serious, just like she used to when I was in the shit at school, just before 'the talk'.

"Lawrence, sometimes the world sends us off course." She squeezes my hand tighter.

"You've just been set adrift, son. The tide's carried you out to sea. I know you'll get back. There's something else I know, you're going to be fine. Maybe not now, but some time in the future. You care about others. That's what makes you a good person." She looks out of the window, gathering her words and as I wait, I'm wondering if she's fighting to believe that.

She turns back. "You always used to fret. You hated injustice. It used to wind you up, even if it wasn't aimed at you. Ever since you were little in primary school. Remember that day you came home with a gouge right down the side of your face because someone had picked on Aiden?"

I grin. "Yes, snotty Aiden."

"The teacher called me in because you took the law into your own hands when the other boy wasn't told off for it. You got into a stupid fight," she said, shaking her head.

"Mrs something," I said. "She had her favourites and snotty wasn't one of them."

"Lawrence!" She sighed in frustration. "It was anyone and everyone on the street. It was always about fairness with you. Aiden probably walked away from the whole thing and forgot about it the next day. You! You end up in detention. But you care."

I hold her gaze and smile. " 'Course I do, Mum. And, I'm going to try and do right, you know? I'm ..."

She raises a hand to hush me.

"I'm proud of how you've coped through this. I'm shocked; still can't believe it. That you could harm someone like that and Rich, of all people. Rich?"

BALANCE

Her words hang in the air, then seep through my flesh and burn at my core from Harrie's betrayal.

I bite my lip so hard it's going to burst out the vitriolic words I'm desperate to contain.

Then she says, "I know it was the drugs. They turn people into what they're not, do foolish, irresponsible things. I know how powerful they can be. I was a nurse, remember? I've seen what happens, that's why I was so worried when I first suspected..."

She stops and waves her hand in irritation. "Anyway, that's all in the past."

I hold still, keep with her, right on track.

"But what happened, it wasn't all your fault, Lawrence. Sometimes life is like that. When you leave this place, you have a right to live your life and you've got your whole life ahead of you now, son."

She shakes her head and there's pleading in her voice. "Lawrence – don't squander it."

I'm listening and waiting as she glances around the room searching for her words.

"What I'm trying to say is – don't let the past dictate your future. What you were and what happened should be left here. When you're released, leave the past here. And that includes the drugs."

I pick up her words and store them away somewhere safe in my head, for keeps.

She smiles and shrugs with satisfaction, like, job done.

I guess she's been waiting to say that to me for the past three years and now we're on our own, she's had the freedom, the space to go for it.

"I've agreed to have a meeting with Rich," I tell her because I know she'll be pleased. "It's a part of this rehab programme to help people sort stuff out, see things a bit more clearly. It's not going to be easy. I know that, Mum."

She raises her brows and beams.

"That's so good to hear, son."

She knows not to talk about Harrie or Rich or that night. She's just pleased and I'm happy that for once I can send her away with something to hang on to.

We talk for a couple of hours. It's the longest session I've ever had during visiting and it's transporting me away, making me feel good. I'm remembering that caring from when I was a kid and it's giving optimism, hope.

Then the bell rings and Mum makes a move to go.

"I've left a package of your favourite things with the warden. I dare say it'll find its way to your room by this evening. Some games magazines, there're so many of them nowadays, newsagents' shelves are full of them. No idea which one to get! So I just put a half a dozen in. Oh and a journal. I used to keep one when I was at college. Sometimes I open it and it's geriatric, I know, but it's good to think about the people I've met and things I've done. I thought you might..." She picks up her bag. "Well, it's all wrapped up for you. Hope – you write something, it was your strength..." She shrugs.

"Journal, eh? OK. I'll think about it, Mum. And thanks for the mags and stuff. You rock," I declare.

She smiles. "There's something else, news about Harrie but..."

She sees my reaction, ponders then changes her mind.

"Not now." I am backing off from the table.

BALANCE

She shakes her head and smiles. "Yes, I know. I'll see you again soon."

We leave it there.

"I hope Dad wins the marathon. Are you going to watch?"

"I'll stand on the pavement somewhere along the route, no doubt," she says, indifferently. "See you next weekend, son. Take care of yourself. Not long and you'll be out and living a proper responsible grown-up life."

"No worries," I say with a goodbye peck.

As I walk back to Peters' wing I feel grounded.

The scales are rising minute by minute and I'm feeling a whole lot lighter.

Until I reach my open door. I suddenly remember, I didn't lock up, bad move. But I did close it, click, click.

I always keep my room tidy; it's been a big part of my survival in here, making sure all's OK, everything neatly placed in its own tiny space, like me.

My eyes rest on the compost and remnants of Walter's plant. It's been torn to shreds, literally: fragments of green, pink and mauve are mashed into chunks of black earthy shit strewn across my carpet, bed and chair.

Harrie's letters have been tossed around the room, some torn, others crumpled into heaps and stamped into the compost.

"Christ!"

It's like shitting Armageddon.

The door slams shut behind me and I turn to see Walter. He's standing there. His face is purple, fit to burst; beads of sweat are rolling down his pug nose. His eyes are wild, rolling and he's got this stupid gurgling laugh.

He's actually laughing in my face. My right fist is clenched. I'm about to punch the stupid sucker's lights out.

"What the fuck's going on?"

He's grunting at me like some gorilla, and dribbling.

And I don't know whether to knock him out cold or call the medics.

"You're a bastard, that's what's going on. You're nothing but a cruel, two-faced, evil bastard."

"Hey man, for Christ's sake what's happened?"

I step back in shock. It's not Walter, it's not the same guy who lives next door to me. This is some psycho!

"You told them. You told them I was a pushover. They blabbed everything. You told them I'd grow for them. You told them I was easy, man, easy. You said I'd be their fucking gardening faggot."

He steps up, his fists clenched, his beetroot head cocked to one side.

"That's shit, Walter. I never talked to anyone about you. I'd never do that. Don't be a stupid loser and see what they're doing. They're playing you like a fiddle, man. Listen, don't let them do this crap to you."

I can't believe the power of their poison. Walter's literally foaming at the mouth.

I need to calm him down, to let him know that nothing's changed; it's me, just as I always was, on the level, straight up.

I step up closer.

"You stinking liar. You told them I was a joke, Woods said you told him I was up for their little project 'cause I gave you that. You agreed a cut, some spare for your shitting pocket."

Walter's shaking hand is pointing at the remnants of my plant.

"No way, Walter. Come on, man, get real! I don't mouth off like that. If there's one thing I've always been it's on the level with you, on the level."

I reach towards him to ease him down. I'm worried about him, genuinely concerned for the idiot. I shrug, easy-like to calm him.

But his big fat arms shove me so hard that I crash over my chair, sending it and me rolling against the wall.

The impact of the cold wall slamming into the back of my ribs winds the hell out of me. The pain flashes through momentarily. I shake my head and get my act together quick.

But Walter's already there. He's standing over me, spitting in my face. "Don't fucking push me, Lawrence. You creep."

He crouches and I back into the wall, not through fear. I'm not scared for me – I'm scared for him. He's deranged.

He pulls up his sleeve and shows me a blood-stained tattoo. It's fresh. The flesh on his arm is still risen and scarlet filled with the blue ink of a snake coiled around the letters X H carved deep into his skin.

"See this? Look!" he commands as he rams his fat arm at my face. "I'm one of them now. I know who my friends are now, you sad shit. They're my family. Blood family. Get it? No one can hurt me because they'll mash them for me, including you." But he's crying, sobbing, and his tears are falling right on to my shitting face.

"OK. Walter, I get it, I see, I get it. You're cool, you're cool."

He stands up straight and steps back, ramming his big dirty boots into Harrie's letters on the mud.

"Stay out of my way, Lawrence. From now on keep out of my space, you lowlife piece of shit, or you're dead meat. Just one word from me and you're history." He opens the door and throws a bullet: "Dickhead."

I lie back with my head on the filthy carpet, dazed: stunned by the sudden psycho crack in Wally's personality.

I wonder, I wonder what would have happened if I'd tried, if I'd taken on the crew.

I lay there, looking at the carnage around my room. I think, what if?

Then I know.

It was Walter, or me.

Down, down I sink under those sudden weights.

CHAPTER 12

Amy's standing in my doorway, eyeing me as I sit at my desk, amidst total wreckage.

Yeah, it's pretty obvious someone's freaked out and I don't look like it was me. I glance up then, avert my gaze in case I give too much away.

This guy's seasoned; he knows the deal.

"Right, Lawrence," he says, "better tell me what's happened here then."

I can see he's surprised as his experienced eyes scan the room, measuring things up.

"I had an accident, sir. I'm about to clean it up," I say.

He smirks.

"No. Sorry, son. Not this time. I need to put this on report and you need to come with me."

He gestures to the corridor, rattles his belt keys and escorts me out, locking my door behind us.

He scrutinises me with a flash of disappointment as I'm frogmarched down to the viewing office.

OK. We've got a pretty even relationship, but he's still on the outside and I'm on the in.

Amy walks into the glass fishbowl and quietly, calmly, shuts the door behind us.

"Incident form please, Penny," he says to the other warden.

She gives me an irritated glance and flicks open a drawer, then hands the printed sheet to Amy.

"Call Will and get him up to cover. We'll be in the interview room," instructs Amy.

"Right." Amy turns to me and looks annoyed as hell. "Follow me, sunshine."

The interview room is just what it is: a table, a few chairs and a window on to the back kitchens where the food is delivered for the day.

He kicks back his chair, commands me to sit opposite with a dismissive gesture and proceeds to fiddle with files and notes on the table.

How am I going to get out of this mess? Tricky!

If I tell him what happened with Walter, I'm screwed. His new little friendship group will cut me to shreds.

My mind's racing. There's a whole load of stuff going on around me and I'm getting sucked down the tube.

Mum, I'd promised: no more trouble, no more and then there's the truth and I wonder – will I ever be able speak it again? Life's muzzled me good and proper.

"Right then! I can't let that kind of vandalism and damage occur on my watch. Do you understand what I'm saying? Bin the accident version and don't take the piss, Lawrence. I've got better things to do with my time than listen to your fairy tales," he says, as he fills my name in on the top of the form.

He examines my file and jots down the date of my transfer, checks his watch and pops the time on the form too.

I'm no more than a mark on the paper. I'm just a printed sheet of tick, cross, tick, shit.

"Let's start over, shall we?" he says.

"It wasn't an accident," I state.

He smiles and shakes his head like I've just said the most ridiculous thing in the world.

He sits and waits, glaring at me, pushing me to fill the silence. He's immense, powerful, I can see that now. His imposing presence is bearing down on me and the pressure is hammering into my chest.

I start twitching; my foot's kicking at the other ankle under the table, painful, sharp.

"I lost my temper," I say quickly. My voice comes over feeble, unconvincing.

"Who else was involved? What's the name or names of the others?" he demands. His voice is deeper, sharper. "Woods?"

I can see he's not going to take any prisoners on this one.

"No one."

He sighs and cups his mouth in his palms. He's getting one hell of an aggravated with me. He sits, outraged, his eyes narrow as he scrutinises me like he can see right through to the bone and I'm starting to kick my feet harder under the table.

I escape his glare: look down at my joggers, study the stitching on the pocket while I struggle to think.

My mind's clicking into gear, dealing with the shock, the issue.

Think, Lawrence, why did this happen? I hear that voice in my head commanding me to sort the shit, stay cool, take control.

Then, it comes.

"My mum, she came to visit today. I'd bought that pot plant for her. I paid Walter for it. See, the old man's playing the field and Mum won't cut him adrift. It's pissing me off. So, Mum and me we talked about all the crap that's been going on at home. I've been worried about her. It's been bad for a long time now. She's pill popping. Anyway, she came on her own today, just to talk about it, and I thought I'd handled it. But as soon as I got back to my room – I realised I forgot to give her the friggin plant. I'd been keeping it alive, keeping it going until she came. When she left without it and all we'd talked on – I lost it, trashed the thing. It was just a plant, no real harm done, I thought ..."

I'd cracked it. I'd shifted his target.

"Nothing to do with Walter or Woods, then?" he asks.

"Walter? No way man, nothing. My folks and all that. It screws me up sometimes, that's the sad reality."

He purses his lips, unconvinced. He's rattled that I'm taking him into Fantasyland. He sits for a moment, deciding where to take it, whether to push me, or back off.

"You sure that's where you're setting this? You just lost your head and vandalised your room?" he says quickly. "There will be penalties for you and you alone if you stick to this and you'll have to see your key-worker to work it through. Not good form so close to your out."

I nod. "That's the way it is," I confirm.

I can still feel a dull ache in my ribs from where Walter sent me reeling. I could take him down too, but, I figure, I haven't got the time. He's not worth shit and he's got dark shadows following.

Amy starts writing down all the lies that I've tossed in his direction. His hand moves faster and faster across the page. He holds the pen clumsily between his index finger and his thumb, like writing's not his natural habit.

His fingers flick the pen, tick, cross, tick, cross, tick.

"OK. Sign this then," he says, shoving the report across to me with a sigh.

I unknot my feet as I feel the relief wash over me.

I grab the sheet and pen he's tossed down and go to sign.

"Read it first, Lawrence," he booms. "For Christ's sake, you don't just sign things without reading. Haven't you learnt anything since you've come in here?"

He stamps his hand down on the table and I jump, eyes wide in shock at his rebuke.

I sit up straight and make to look like I'm holding my note of execution and reading it letter by letter, but I'm not seeing the words. I'm playing the game, the lying game.

"Yes, sorry, sir."

He flicks his hand. "Ahh, you lot are all the same, empty-headed, don't bother your arses to think for yourselves. There's too much work in thinking. If you thought a little more before you acted..."

I look up. "Then I wouldn't be in here, sir?" I say politely because I know he's riled by me. "I get that."

He nods while I silently conclude, 'And you wouldn't have a shit job like this without me either, sir."

See, it's an eco system sir, and someone's got to be right at the bottom of that chain.

CHAPTER 13

I opted for cleaning the showers instead of rec night and it's not so bad.

OK, so there's hair, gunge, soap and curlies, and other stuff I'm not about to guess at, sloshing around in the foot-wells. But the indomitable Officer Pevensey smiled sweetly, loaded me up with latex and heavy-duty kit, bar and oxygen mask, to help me handle the shit.

I finish my stint at the end of the week, then dues are paid once again. Pity though, I haven't had the chance to see Lewis. I got his smart-arsed note under my door three days after the stint.

'Hey, Mrs Mop, you trashed your room? Joy! Parting gift, mate. Shave's got a fresh pack of baccy, want some?'

I smiled when I got that one. He keeps me buoyed.

I'm still shaken when I think of Walter. The extra cleaning duties have kept me off the floor and out of his sights all week and, more importantly, him out of mine, which has to be a genuine bonus.

But when I think of Walter, I think life's a real bitch. Not for me, I can handle a meltdown from the sad weirdo.

BALANCE

But he's been hijacked. He's one poor bastard who's never going to be free, even on the outside. He's property now. He's anyone's who'll have the power to control and own him.

Jesus, that's sad!

On Friday, the luscious Amar joins me in the laundry queue.

Amar keeps telling everyone he was a male model destined for the New York runway – that was until he strangled his mother, literally speaking.

He's six three and a lean machine.

He walks like an Egyptian cat, like his feet never leave the tiled floor; he just glides silently, effortlessly along in his wide Aladdin cottons. Give him his dues, the guy's got style, panache.

He's OK, is Amar. In fact he's a real character, but he's dark on the inside too, man.

He walks with his nose in the air and craves one thing: attention. Whether he gets his fix by abuse from other inmates or just simple curiosities about his behaviour and his sentence, it's all something to savour for him; he's a tabloid gossip junky. He's a real hoot.

"Hi, handsome!" He nestles in beside me.

I smile and clutch my laundry tote closer to my leg, to take the piss!

"Clean boy, aren't you? That's pretty full," he says, glancing down at my bag and giving me a furtive wink.

"Yes, Amar, I don't stink like half the monkeys in this dump," I reply, looking up into the boy's brown eyes.

He sniggers. "Darling, monkeys? That's far too high an order of species for this lot."

I grin.

"So, did you hear it all kick off in my room, three a.m. on Wednesday?" he asks.

"Yes, I heard all right, Amar."

And I had. I'd heard the wardens racing to Amar's room with the medic on their heels. I heard the shouting, the panic and the doors slamming and I can tell you, I was seriously peeved.

You see, Amar's a diabetic and he plays games with his insulin and sugar levels just to keep those wardens on their toes and, boy, doesn't he make them dance.

The uniforms watch him like hawks; he makes them nervous as shit. I suppose it's power for Amar, in a macabre, satisfying kind of way.

"Coma," he says. "I drank a glass of the coolest coke in the world and was out of it, darling. Only wish I'd seen the look on the sad bastard's faces."

"'Crazy," I say, not wishing to encourage such dangerous foolhardiness for entertainment; it's not my bag.

"Oh, for Christ's sake! Sweetie, what else has a boy to do with himself in this zoo? Or maybe you've got some suggestions, Lawrence?"

He gazes down at me with his intense, chestnut-brown eyes and gives an exaggerated smouldering stare. I'm not moved, merely amused.

"Well, you could try eating properly and cruising over to the activities area," I say.

"Oh boring old you. I'm not interested in the kind of activities listed in their cheap hand-outs. No, do you know?" He purses his lips and holds the moment for effect.

"Hmmmm, I'll just have to hit on your friend, Lewis. He's quite a looker, lovely strong jawline. Not the gorgeous locks and sexy charisma you possess, sweetie. But he'll do. What do you say? Getting jealous? You hot-blooded boy."

I laugh. The thought of Amar making a play for Lewis fills my head with a multitude of hilarious scenarios; life can be fun.

"I always thought you two were an item and maybe I could, uh hum, make it a threesome?" he suggests. But I'm not offended. I know he's tormenting, playing games. I play back, I don't feel threatened and he knows it.

"Give it a go, Amar. I don't have rights over Lewis," I encourage, unable to resist a satisfied grin.

"Oh stop it, how exquisite," says Amar.

No one really knows exactly why Amar's inside. Rumour has it that he strangled his mother. Whether he killed her or not is up for debate. I suspect not, given his wrist width. I'd go for attempted myself.

The murder story was probably something Amar spread about for more infamy. But he's outrageous, fun, and to me that makes life in this hellhole a little more interesting and hence tolerable.

There's a vulnerable, human quality to Amar, something that sets him apart, makes me feel a connection and a skewed respect. I keep my own vulnerability hidden deep, that's essential, for obvious reasons, but he's out there with it, man. So respect.

"I'm going to give those soldiers a week," he says, "then I'll hit them with an iced bun and a couple of cupcakes. They would have cut back on night watches by then, relaxed a bit.

My God, if I can't relax in this menagerie, why should they?" Amar chuckles and shrugs.

"Not in the early hours, please, Amar. I have problems enough sleeping," I moan.

"Ohh boo hoo," he mocks.

"Don't you ever get scared? Don't you ever think you're not going to come out of this alive? Come out of the fit?" I ask, stressing my bewilderment at the insanity.

"But that's the whole point, sweetie," he says nonchalantly. "I don't care if I never wake up again. What a sweet ending. Divine!"

I shrug and accept life or death is his right, his decision. But I can't understand it.

Life is pretty dark, I see that, but there's a part at the core of my being that insists I value life, no matter what.

Still, I'm not in Amar's skin, wearing his life.

Being Amar could suck so much I'd want to go out in a sugar rush too. But it would take a lot to get me to that emotional place.

And there's a part of me that believes he's bluffing. I'm sure, deep down, that he wants to live just like the rest of us losers in this place. Amar is the greatest of the great pretenders.

When Amar first came in, he was placed under constant observation, not only because of his fluctuating sugar levels but also from the constant risk of attack at the hands of the homophobes.

They succeeded a couple of times in doing him over. I'd see him around the block sporting black eyes, thick lips, gouges down his cheeks and, when it got really bad, he suffered the humiliation of stitches and a faggot inscription on his neck.

It took a long time for the uniforms to get that off his skin and I reckon for the pain in him to fade.

But Amar continued to drift down the corridors like a freaking supermodel, a battered, serene supermodel.

That's what I like about Amar, he's freakin irrepressible. In fact, the more they hammer him down, the taller the guy stands.

I dump my laundry tote and we head over to the canteen.

"Oh, there he is," says Amar, with a naughty chuckle. He's pointing at Lewis, who's standing waiting for me with his filled dinner tray.

Lewis' eyebrows rise in horror and he mouths the word 'Shit' at me as he dives for an end seat at a table.

I grab my tray and queue with Amar on my tail.

"Boiled testicles again, oh dear," declares Amar. He sighs as they slop a spoonful of meatballs on to my spaghetti.

"Watch it, potty mouth," says the female supervisor. She's holding the ladle and her tattooed fingers are primed ready to slap some food on to Amar's empty plate and into his Adonis face. The jabberwocky's been known to do it to many a feckless diner.

"I'm doing salad instead. But thank you, so much," stresses Amar, grandly prising the plate from her unyielding chubby fingers.

He heads to the salad counter, floating with a regal air.

Someone wolf-whistles and Amar waves dismissively.

I gravitate to the seat opposite Lewis and catch sight of Walter. He's striding in with Woods and a group of

Neanderthals. Walter's stance is different: he swaggers now and eyes up the nervies and the newbies with sadistic pleasure.

The queue shifts and visibly disintegrates as Woods and his merry men head to the front.

"Asshole," I curse.

Lewis glances round, then back at me. "What's been going on? Why did they shove you on pube duties? I'd heard you'd trashed things, had a meltdown in your cell. Tell you, I was a tad worried, but then I realised it was all balls and you'd surface clean. It's not your style."

"Walter psyched in my friggin room, wrecked the place," I hiss.

"Thought you two were sound," he states, with a touch of smugness.

"Yeah, well, he's keeping different company now. That's just the way it turned out. But it nearly got me points on my card, man. Amy had me well in his sights," I moan.

"I did warn you. That kid's nothing but a baby. Give him a dummy and he'll suck it up from anyone," says Lewis, shoving another mouthful in.

I reflected silently and came to appreciate Lewis' wisdom.

"You off duties now? I'm getting bored shitless. I've been running on the treadmill just to get the adrenalin going all sodding week," says Lewis.

"Yeah?" I laugh and warn, "Better practise speed walking my friend, Amar's got the hots for you. I told him you were up for it." I blow a kiss.

"Get stuffed, Lawrence," says Lewis, snorting, "You're a shitting comedian."

I laugh with satisfaction as Lewis glances nervously back, checking Amar's table.

Amar spots Lewis and returns a smouldering look.

"Christ!" hisses Lewis. "You're shitting serious!"

I grin and realise I've ticked another week off my time. I also know Lewis is a rock-solid friend and I'm going to miss his company big time.

CHAPTER 14

Dear Rich,

I've spoken to the wardens. They're arranging a meeting. Mr Gregory's going to let me know when you want one.

I don't know what to say just now.

The first time I read your letter, it was three in the morning. I don't sleep too well either. Now I keep reading it again and again and each time, it hurts just as much as the first time. It hurts not because of me, but because of you. That's the truth.

Lawrence

CHAPTER 15

Walter's getting cocky. He swaggers down the corridor, slams doors in people's faces and has turned into more of an obnoxious little shit than he ever was.

He's coming near to the end of his term. There might have been a time when he would have walked out into the big wide world and stood a chance of being happy. Now I know, it was never meant to be.

He's hooked on the high of the crew. Their power, intimidation and predilection for cruelty is his security; the thrill of being a part of some bigger force, even if it is a crock of shit, is too much for the pea-brain to resist.

He's setting up to connect with the outside crew as well. The fact that he's grown the stuff inside has given him real street cred; Walter's a regular dude, a cock of the rock, a real Clever Trevor.

The crazy thing is that when he's out – he's still going to be trotting back here to Her Majesty's every week with little packages for the crew inside, doing the stuff. Until he gets caught, and I know he will.

Sucker!

Maybe I shouldn't think about it. Shit happens. The scales tip one way or the other for us all. But it's the discovery of life's delicate balance that scares the hell out of me.

I'm trying to get my head around the meeting with Rich when another letter arrives from Harrie. I add it to my now crumpled, blackened wodge, which I've locked in my drawer in my table. I'm a quick learner!

I've opened Mum's journal. It's clean, lined, virgin white paper. Good quality. The book is classy, leather-bound with a blue ribbon marker. I can't believe she can still waste her money on good quality stuff for such a bad quality son.

Where the hell do I start?

Maybe at the beginning? Yes, that's where I'll start. My hand hovers over the page. 'Write, Lawrence, write.'

But I can't! I'm frozen. My head's full of emptiness peering down at a slab of white.

Then I think, so long as I mark the paper, you know, stain it with ink, that'll break the spell.

So I doodle a picture of a boat. It's a tugboat like the one I used to see on the morning show when I was a shrimp. The little tug's got a chimney and smoke puffing out and there's a stickman, that's me, driving and there's another stickman wearing a sailor hat. He's saluting at the bow. That's Lewis and we're sailing the seven seas and we're free and it's worked and I start my story, at the beginning.

Mum told me I shouldn't have been a Lawrence, she was going to call me William, but her friend, Gwyneth, the other nurse who worked with her on the ward, had her son first and nabbed the Prince's name. So Mum opted for Lawrence because of D.H. Lawrence. I've never read his work, maybe

BALANCE

one day, who knows? Christ, Mum kind of fancied the guy's middle name, too, of Herbert, but Dad put his foot down. Thanks for that one, Dad.

I wonder if maybe I'd been named a William, my life would have been different. Perhaps your name determines your fate. Who knows? Say, if I was a Harlequin or a Siegfried, yeah, or Albert, I'd be a shitting genius. Anyway, I digress.

Fate, yeah and Harrie. You see, only we know what she did. And what Harrie did puts me in a bad, bad place, deep inside. She could have changed everything, the whole scene. She had the power. Shit, there was a part of Harrie I never knew existed, not until...

I wonder if some nights she's sitting up like me, looking out at the black canvas, and remembering and suffering in her own torment.

Sometimes I wish I was Lewis or even Amar, for Christ's sake. But no, I'd rather be dead than be Walter, poor bastard.

Me and Harrie. Harrie the big sister; she always looked out for me. Always there, like I was her baby more than I was Mum's. I worshipped Harrie. I loved her.

There's a knock on my open door. I drop the pen, feeling guilty and why, Christ knows.

It's Amy. A part of me figures the knock signifies respect. He's acknowledging my personal space and I know that he doesn't have to. I really appreciate it. Like I say, perspectives change when you're inside; the little things matter.

"Morning, sunshine," he says. "Letter from the services."

I sit tight and hold out my hand and he raises a brow like I'm crazy. I get the point: get off my lazy little arse.

"Sorry, sir," I say. I hop up and respectfully take it from him.

"Studies?" he says, handing me the envelope. He nods at my journal.

"Uh, yes, English Lit," I say quickly.

"Hah, brave lad. I never was that way inclined at school, found reading and writing gave me a headache and the only cure was sport. Some of us aren't wired for it. Brains work differently. You stick in." He gives me the thumbs up and takes off.

I wander back to my desk and open the envelope. It's from Gregory and it's official all right.

FAO: Mr Lawrence Somers.

Young offenders are offered assistance in resettling effectively through a range of voluntary and statutory agencies including: Department of Works and Pensions seconded staff, C.R.I. who offer a housing advisory service and officers trained by NACRO providing advice on housing-related issues combined with the local employment agency within the region/area in which the YO is to resettle. As a part of this ongoing service, both named parties have instructed the SORI agency:

Mr Richard Grove:

Of: 1, Pensford Avenue, Bristol, Avon BS21 3IU

& The serving party:

Mr Lawrence Somers,

Her Majesty's Young Offenders Institution Hendbrook.

To meet with the facilitator:

Mr P Gregory

Department for Rehabilitation Services,
Unit 28
Hendbrook
On the 27th July 2013 at 2 p.m.

Meeting to be held at the offices of HMYOI Hendbrook at 2p.m.

Both parties are to confirm their booked appointment to Mr Gregory by no later than the 20th July on the contact number below.

SORI
Tel: 0863 499187

So, this is it, set like the ten friggin commandments, thou shalt not bottle out, thou shalt not let Mum down. No going back – and I'm thinking I've only got a short while to put my emotional armour on for this meeting.

Why the hell did they arrange the appointment so quickly? I've been in here for nearly three years. And what am I going to say to the guy? Will I tell Rich what really happened that night? He won't remember, I'm sure of that. Christ, he had his skull smashed in, his body shattered. He was in a coma for a month.

No!

Shit! What's he planning to say to me? Maybe Rich knows I'm nearing the end of my term and he's instigated this meeting. Yeah, that figures, but I still don't know why, what or how?

Rich wasn't a shit, he wasn't spiteful or venomous; but time and trauma changes people. He'd probably be a completely different animal now. Understandable that he should hate my sad little guts. After what happened, Rich should be dead. But he survived and it's the one thing that's kept those scales off the floor for me. The only light that's shining in this stinking world is that Rich is still alive ...

CHAPTER 16

So I'm on day release. They're dispatching me to see some social and employment guy to discuss training for a future. Problem is – I'm still kind of locked in the past.

I've got a list of gets for Lewis and Amar, so I make sure the note's tucked in where I don't forget it.

OK. I'm up for buying the special Dune chocolate bars and Excess energy drinks for Lewis. He's ordered twenty-four of those shitting bars, which is what he'll be doing when he's piled them back.

He reckons he's going to ration them out three a month until his release day. Yeah? Now that's willpower!

But Amar wants me to get him a bottle of nail varnish, with some weird name like butternut squash or frigging fruit salad, and he insisted it's got to be the right shade with some stupid eyeshadow to match.

He's off his trolley. No, I'm off my trolley for agreeing to go on his mission.

"You're such a lucky boy, a day all to yourself outside with proper human beings. Well, I saw these in the latest Vogue, Lawrence. Divine! I'll be eternally indebted to you if you pick them up," he says, thrusting the tattered glossy ad into my hand.

"Ah, Amar, mate. I wouldn't know where to look," I plead.

"You're a smart boy, darling. Just head for the perfume counter and those gorgeous babes will show you where to go. You never know, you might actually enjoy it," he says.

Right, so what universe is he cruising in? I stuff the cash into my pocket, but suspect I will not humiliate myself with the babes in the chemist unless my brain short-circuits.

So here I am, sitting in a minibus with one other guy and it's like we're off on a seaside outing, happy little schoolboys.

I don't think so!

This outing means I have to book in at the local police station for tabs, then it's appointments with youth employment and back for transport to Hendbrook for five p.m. Being late's a no-goer or privileges are cut.

This town isn't my patch. I was transferred to Hendbrook from the courtroom near my home after the conviction.

I've never seen the surrounding area; it's weird living somewhere for nearly three years and not knowing what's on the other side of a wall. After a while inside, you start to believe that the whole of outside is just a map of corridors, blocks and concrete.

As we drive towards the station, I look out at fields. They're so neatly ploughed, I decide they remind me of folds of chocolate, or maybe I've just got Lewis' Dune bars on the brain.

But then another field comes into view. It's brimming with yellow blooms tipping over the edge of the hillside and into the distance.

BALANCE

I lean back and enjoy the view.

Turbine sails glint silver in the sunlight as they sweep in circles.

The world looks beautiful out, but inside, mine is full of ugliness.

It's stunning out here. Looking out of the window I had no idea, as we drove through those gates today, of the new world that was waiting to greet me.

It's only having all this denied that makes me, for the first time in my self-indulgent, conceited little life, appreciate it.

Soon that small part of me, the little boy, does begin to feel like he's on his special seaside outing.

I soak up the warmth through the glass and look across at my fellow traveller. He's about my age, skinny as hell, but wiry, able to take care of himself.

He's sitting oblivious to my presence, just gazing out. Seems like he's got a headful of thoughts and memories too.

Then that warm feeling inside turns cold. The blackness surfaces from somewhere in the deep recesses of my mind. It's the motion, the growl of the diesel engine, it brings it all back: taking me on that first traumatic journey from the court cells to Hendbrook.

The past kicks its ugly boot right into the present.

It was very late that night. A fifteen-year-old boy was sitting wondering what had happened to his life. I'd been stuck in the cell all afternoon and most of the early evening. There'd been a lot of kicking off around me in other cells, angry shouts, then long periods of painful silence.

I remember resting my chin on my knees, huddling into myself and fighting to shut out the hollering, the slams and keys ringing out. Man, they must have had one busy day. I guessed they'd forgotten about me, all the long hours of the afternoon. My belly was growling for food and churning with emotion.

Suddenly my cell door opened and some faceless uniform stepped inside. He didn't bother his arse to speak, just indicated for me to move myself and pronto. He escorted me down the corridor, out of the heavy back doors and into a courtyard where a police van was waiting, engine running.

It was surreal, like someone else was going through the motions, my avatar in another game.

I wondered where Mum, Dad and Harrie were. They'd splintered off, become a kind of different family: respectable strangers.

They would have left after the verdict early in the afternoon. Mum was sobbing. That really cut me up, that I did that to her.

Harrie's face just turned to stone. I looked at her and she stared back. Those eyes, they were filled with something I'd never seen in her before. It rocked me to the core.

And Dad? I could see the dick just wanted to get Mum and Harrie out of there. He had each hand on their shoulders, driving away the pain I'd inflicted on them all. He glanced back at me, yeah – I remember that! It was the 'Sorry, son, but you had this coming' look.

Then they disappeared and took my old life with them. Like I was out of their lives, for good.

That verdict transformed me into another person, a criminal with a GBH on my record. My legs shuffled me along like some goon behind the uniform to the van. I kept repeating in my head the mantra, 'It's OK. Lawrence, you're going to wake up and find this is a bad dream. It's that shit candy you took, it's sent you to Terrorsville.' Then there was the hope for a call, "Stop! Big cock-up, it's not him. Not *that* Lawrence."

Looking out of the shaded windows of the transport, I wasn't handcuffed. I wondered back then, why? Like, a GBH is a serious charge, right? Why didn't they put the danger tab on me?

Yeah, no confusion on that question when they escorted an older guy into the van: the genuine article. That's the first time I confronted some heavy shit and knew the next three years of my life was going to be the real survival course.

Christ! He was frightening. His long greasy hair was tied in a side ponytail. He must have had tattoos from his arse to his head. All ugly stuff, words and images, all 'I hate mankind' shit. He was linked to some burly copper opposite and was being transported forty miles further on to HMP Psycholand, after my drop.

He had piercing blue eyes; they were long, semi shut, snake-sharp and focused their evil gaze right on me, direct, intense, poisonous. Like he wouldn't stop eyeballing me. I was the magnet, the pull. I thought he was going to rip my throat out.

He rattled those cuffs right up in my face with delight and laughed, the mad bastard.

"Settle down, Petal," the copper said, nonchalant, like this guy wasn't the nastiest, craziest son-of-a-bitch anyone would ever have the misfortune of meeting.

I remember swallowing hard, and resisting the urge to pee on my seat. On the level, I was shell-shocked from the trauma of the court case, and the return for sentencing after Harrie's evidence.

Now, as those images flood back, they fill me with revulsion. But all I could think about when I had crazy up close was welcome to your life, Lawrence; there're going to be a hundred more Petals where you're going, son.

Petal must have relished having the white-shirted middle-class dweeb sitting across from him. I bet our brief encounter filled him with joy.

I also remember the Youth Officer booking me in on arrival at HMYOI giving the transport driver a hefty grilling for carrying a minor with Petal.

"Sorry, mate, short staffed and the direct was to transport both prisoners today," said nonchalant.

I guess he thought it would be a baptism by fire for Yours Truly.

I guess he was right.

That was the night, as I lay awake in the observation room, before going down to my cell next morning, that I swore I would never see Harrie again. The day she gave evidence against me was the day I sentenced her out of my life, for good. Not, I concluded, that losing me would have been much of a loss to her.

So, I'm looking at my official slip and there's that same old tag line: 'Expected outcomes.'

Expected outcomes:

A discussion with the relevant personnel on retraining with a view to future employment.

BALANCE

Connection with local authorities and support services within the area the party intends to take up residence upon release.

A clear programme outlined for the final weeks of term for rehabilitation and resettlement.

To which I add, twenty-four choccy bars for Lewis and the friggin nail varnish and eyeshadow for Amar Tootsville.

Then it hits me like a kick in the balls. 'Cause I'm standing on the steps of the police station, booked in, registered out, clutching my map and instructions but I have not the slightest clue of what I'm freakin doing.

My travel companion, Wiry, sidles out of the police door after me and hovers. We both survey the traffic, the rush, the people, like it's some strange pantomime.

"All right, man?" he grunts.

I don't know him. He's not been on my wing, but he seems OK.

"Sure, no worries," I say.

"Cheers. See you for the fun ride back," he says with a smirk.

"Yeah." I watch him walk off and disappear into the crowd.

Only, I'm standing there like some abandoned child wondering where the hell I am, where have all these people have come from, and why won't someone tell me what to do?

I kind of follow my travel companion, but he's well out of sight by now.

As I walk my head spins. I seem to have developed some form of vertigo. Not nice!

I wander for a while, this way, that way. I avert my eyes from the glances of others. I can't look at anyone. They might see me for what I am. I stand and stare vacantly in shop windows at books, hardware, clothing, mobile phones, even at an optician's shades display.

I'm getting a weird kind of anxiety: like I'm treading along an invisible platform and about to topple. Gotta keep my balance.

I head on further and find myself stepping into a chemist shop. Sure, a chemist, that's what I wanted, wasn't it? I pull out Amar's advert and tentatively go to a counter.

It's like I'm on remote control. I'm a robot readjusting, reconfiguring and reprogrammed to perform this weird task.

There's a woman wearing a white overall and an orange face. Her black-lined eyes crease deeper as she watches me approach her counter. I think she knows I'm a criminal. She knows I'm a good-for-nothing little shit. I can't look her in the face.

I retrieve my scrunched up advert and pass it over the counter to her with a grunt.

Why did I do this? Why did I come in here?

I realise, I was instructed to. I was directed, step by painful step, by Amar. Move by humiliating move I was given specific commands and I come to the disturbing conclusion that I have become institutionalized.

"We've got the nail varnish in stock, but not the eyeshadow. It's such a popular range. Taking a while to get new stock in," she says briskly.

"Oh, I'll have that then," I say, eyeing the patterns on the floor.

BALANCE

"The nail varnish?"

"Yeah, that."

"OK. We've got an eyeshadow shade that's close to the one you want. But this one's not a powder, it's a cream. Minerals are good for the skin, pricey but worth it," she says, digging in some drawer under her counter.

The instructions are clearly written on the ad; it says no to cream, yes to powder. I must keep to the ad or I fail.

"No worries. Just the nail varnish, thanks."

"Well, there's not much difference. It's not the same company, but it's definitely the same shade, maybe a bit lighter," she insists, unscrewing the black top and dipping her finger in. She rubs the sparkle on the back of her hand like some friggin party trick.

Sweat dampens under my hood, the muscles contract around my throat and tighten up in my neck. I want out of this. Music, lights, the smell of heady perfume intensify. I'm going to puke.

"No, nail varnish, that's it," I repeat.

"I can put a bit on your hand to try out the colour," she suggests, shoving her hand over the counter.

"What the f***?" I start in horror, but catch myself. "Sorry, no, I'll just have the stuff in the bottle."

She slams the drawer shut with an irritable tut.

"Suit yourself," she snaps. She holds the bottle across the counter and waits for payment. I feel out of my depth, inadequate.

"Sorry, I've got a note somewhere," I say, as I rummage frantically through my pockets. There're papers, appointments, names, all stamped with HMYOI. I'm stamped with HMYOI. I cough as I draw out the brown crumpled note.

I hand it to her and she unfolds it with obvious repugnance before shoving it into the till and counting out my change.

"Thank you," she says, uninterested.

The tiny bottle of luminous colour is hastily shoved in my back pocket and I stagger towards the exit of the shop like a drunk.

I am damaged and this sudden affirmation of my other self in the real world is crushing. I burst through the doors of the chemist back out into the busy street.

I'm losing my balance again. The scales are dipping gently to the negative. I want to bolt – to head back to the safety of the place I despise, my box.

Mum! She'll be waiting. She knows it's almost time for out. Can't run.

Got to get a grip. The map's open in my hands, so I scan, trying to decipher the directions. This is Tucker Street. Think, think!

I head west and walking calms me again; the pounding in my chest lessens to a gentle beat. There are names on street corners and buildings, matching those on my scrunched-up piece of paper.

I cross the road and head to the river. Soon there comes the steady flow of water. Over the wall, there are birds on the water, coot, moorhen, black-backed gulls. I watch them fighting for scraps or bobbing on the glinting surface. Reddish foam gathers and bubbles along the bank, catching the city's

BALANCE

debris, sweeping it up and allowing the flow of fresher water to carry through. In the drink, there's life, clear, natural, undiscriminating.

I watch and listen to life.

My vertigo is easing. I'm finding my feet; rebalancing. I determine which way to head. The offices are a distance away. Shit, I've wandered off course. But the physical discomfort has faded and as the employment offices come into view, twenty minutes later, I've realise the blinkers are off. Can't say exactly when it happened, but I've merged with the world, transformed into a small part of humanity and daily life on the outside.

There are some fit girls floating by, prompting a familiar flush of excitement, challenge and anticipation. A pretty brunette actually smiles at me, like she's seen something good. I must be gawping at her like she's a freak show, but she's grinning and is OK about it. I see my reflection in a window and I'm smiling like a loon. There're shoppers, people with pushchairs and toddlers kicking up or playing. It's weird to see so much colour, so many different styles and even weirder, ages. Shit, yeah, there no wrinklies serving in Hendbrook, nothing but screwy guys. The only oldies are staff and you kind of don't see them as ordinary people, right? They're uniforms.

But this, this is neat, suddenly the world is made up of so much more than the problem kids at Hendbrook.

That's kind of stunning.

Later, after an uninspiring appointment with a bored official at the training centre, I emerge from the offices armed with a carrier bag full of useless leaflets promising a glossy future. The bored adviser offers a scrap of idle philosophy: "It's up to you."

Yeah? Really? Well, thanks for nothing. And no, it's not up to me; it's up to the business bribed high enough by the government to take on a juvenile criminal for training.

The remainder of my first taste of freedom is idled away in a computer games shop surfing. Inzane Games was on route back to the police station so it killed an hour for me, reading blurb and cruising under the wary gaze of the sales guy.

Yeah, could have spent an hour in the park or wandering down by the river, but that would have given me time to think, to remember and regret.

So mission to fill my head with crap is successful, somewhere between the Zombie eating machines and the Dinosaur Death Duel.

I book in at the police station and end up sitting on the outside wall for forty minutes waiting for transport back. I'd always imagined my first out as being a hoot, like I'd be so high on the freedom I'd barely get back for transport in time.

I seem to have transformed into some sad bastard.

The minibus is late. Shit! Does that mean I get my balls chewed off at Hendbrook for late return? How does this work? My travel companion paces up and sits further down from me. He's looking chilled. Maybe he's not been in long enough to see the contrast. Some kids only get a few months, a short slap on the hand like Wanker Walter. Mine's up there with the midterms and no matter how young you are – time is time.

"OK?" he says.
"Yeah, OK."

But we both acknowledge through silent disdain that it's not been the experience of a lifetime.

"Trees, man." He shakes his bag of leaflets, "I've just got a bag full of trees." He nods with a cynical grin.

I shake too. "Same as."

We sit and wait, meditating, and I didn't want to do that, too disturbing.

I realise, under the skin, people live different lives; hold other beliefs to those they want me to think they believe. It's all a smokescreen, a magic trick.

Harrie! Harrie! I don't know anyone under the skin.

No more trust.

As that reality seeps through my own skin, the bitterness and the grief fill me up again.

I'm blasted out of the blackness by a car horn. A cab rolls up. The driver leans across and calls, "Hendbrook?"

"Yeah," I say.

We've now progressed from police van to public transport, impressive! As we drive back to Hendbrook, a part of me is wounded, burning from the harsh lesson that I don't fit in the real world like I used to. I've lost three years of my young life. My confidence is at base level. I feel like a loser. Fucking joke's on me.

CHAPTER 17

Nothing ever changes inside.

I come to that sobering conclusion as we drive through the gates of Hendbrook.

We stay locked in, running away from the past like rats on a wheel, but that past stays in our cells with us. That's what makes the cell, the past.

As I walk down the corridors, I notice things I hadn't seen before. There are posters splattered across the walls, more than I remembered, but I'm opening my eyes. I'm looking around and pretending the visitor: doing my make-believe, taking it all in as if for the first time. Mind games, man.

It's simple, as.

But those small changes in my internal perspective keep me sane.

Posters are awash with graffiti, but this graffiti's real art, it's a masterpiece. Then there's classical art, commercial designs, cartoons, it's all cool, impressive. Like people have put in the time, the thought, pinned up a piece of themselves. It means something.

Most are obviously produced by the inmates promoting performances of Shakespeare, films, sports and games.

BALANCE

Others are official, advertising workshops and offering words of wisdom: *Respect others, Respect yourself, Words are Power. Words are the Weapon. Violence is Weakness.* HMYOI, Changing Perspectives.

So how much of my perspective on life has changed? I regret the past, there's no doubt about that, but I also know I'd regret the past whether I am in here or out on the other side. Rich! His suffering: that's pretty heavy stuff, I mean, it's gutting.

I know what happened that night crushed me. But what Harrie did? That destroyed me. OK. Now there's only one person on the out I know I can trust. Mum. I still hold what she said close. I plan, on the out, to make it right. To prove that the belief she has in me is justified and I'll start by talking to her about her future, not just mine.

I'm walking down to my wing and as I approach Howard wing, ISU block, it's locked down, heavily bolted. I hear what's happening inside: shouts, doors slamming, echoes of violence and anger reverberate through the air. That crew haven't read the official posters on the wall. There's no respect, only rage and fear.

CHAPTER 18

When you're inside you believe nothing changes on the outside. Sure, you listen to the news and visitors give updates on what's happening to those we know or don't: the kind of news that fills those awkward silences during visits.

But as I hit my wing, no one is in the viewing booth and I guess they're out on rounds. I saunter past Walter's room. It's strange how it's always empty now. He's someplace else playing with his new friends. Walter's release is either this week or next. I don't give a shit anymore when it is. I'll just be pleased when that little chapter of my life is closed.

I locked the door to my room before I took off in the morning, but I still check and make sure as I continue on to visit Amar.

Amar's lying on his bed, reading a magazine with his door wide open. His room stinks of incense or scented oils. It's heady, sickly and gets right up my nose as I tap on his door, manners and all that. Candles are scattered across the floor and around his narrow bookshelves. How the hell did he manage to talk the uniforms into allowing this set-up?

BALANCE

"Lawrence!" he exclaims, casting his magazine aside and dramatically rising to his feet. "Was it heavenly out there? You must tell me, sweetie. Oh, you are a lucky boy."

"Busy!" I say, failing to hide my obvious disillusionment. "Busy as shit."

"Oh! Come and tell me all about it," he says, patting the seat of his chair.

I smile. "Can't hang around. I've got twenty chocolate bars to offload on to Lewis before they melt in my pocket and I look like I've shit myself." I say it like I'm some kind of delivery service or worse, Lewis' mother. "Here," I announce as I dump the nail varnish on to his table along with his change. "Couldn't get your eyeshadow, though. Sorry!"

I feel like I've just let the girlfriend down.

"Oh, you're a star." Amar sweeps the tiny luminous bottle of colour up into his hand with a passion. He holds it to the window and inspects it. "Oh, Lawrence, spot on. It's *so* this season."

I grin. "Yes, well the babe wasn't quite what I'd anticipated. But I escaped in one piece."

"An old trout, was she?" Amar screws up his nose with mischievous delight.

"Sure, something like that. See you," I say heading out.

He calls to me. "Lawrence!"

I turn and there's genuine warmth and gratitude in his eyes.

"You're quality stuff, my boy," he announces. "A bit special. Thank you."

"Yeah? Special needs all right." I wave and head off to the viewing office. There're lines I don't want to cross with Amar.

125

I rate the guy, he's unique for sure, but I need my space. I hurry to get an area pass so that I can enter Lewis' wing and offload the bars like illegal booty. Amy's not around, but Penny, his colleague, is standing at the cubicle window. She's watching as I approach the door and the odd way she's looking at me makes me think there's something dark coming my way.

My mind goes through a million scenarios as to why I may be facing trouble. Maybe they pipped Lewis and me smoking the baccy at the match? Maybe someone, Walter, has shafted me with the guards, accused me of some shit just to make sure they keep me in for a longer spell. I sense whatever it is – it's not good and the hairs prickle on my arms like a sweep of electricity.

"I didn't see you come back in, Lawrence," says Penny as I enter her fishbowl, but her voice is soft, not accusatory.

"Just went to give something to Amar, it was checked in at the gate," I say, quickly.

But Penny's looking at me like I'm a man facing the gallows and the adrenalin kicks in. "I just need a pass to Lewis' wing. I need to give him something, the bars."

"Leave them with me. I'll make sure he gets them," she says with a reassuring smile and I'm getting more nervous by the second. "I'm afraid you've got a visitor, Lawrence. He's waiting in the interview room. He's been here for some time," she announces.

OK. So now I know there's a problem, a big shitting problem. Like, this is not visiting day, and sessions end at 5.30 weekdays, so what the hell's going on? But maybe it's Gregory. No, can't be, the appointment's already set with Rich.

"What, now? It's after seven. I thought visitors weren't..."

"You'd better come with me," she cuts in, and as she passes me in the doorway she gently squeezes my arm.

I follow her, silently, my heart pounding, my throat tightening until I'm going to choke. Stay cool, I keep repeating, but it's not working. The blood's pumping in my ears, whoosh whoosh. I never could deal with the unknown. If I face a loaded weapon, I can handle it, know what I'm taking on. I face a vacuum? I'm done.

She turns briefly, gives a feeble smile, then opens the door and I go in.

Dad stands up. He's drawn, pale and his eyes are shadowed, hollow. He looks the worst I've seen him in a long time.

"Dad! You're here," I say.

It's a curious line to give your father on an unexpected visit, but everything's out of sync, disconnected, anything I say would be out of context.

"Son," he says, "It's bad." He looks shaken and suddenly the gravity of the situation hits me.

"Take as long as you need," says Penny, as she locks me in for the agony I'm about to face.

"It's your mother. She's had a massive stroke, son. They don't think she's going to make it," blurts Dad.

Dad steps forward, his lips trembling. He reaches out to grasp my shoulder, but I step back. I stare at him in shock. He gazes back, broken, scared.

I can't give him what he wants. I'm not his kid son any more. He cut me loose a long time ago.

He betrayed Mum and has only ever had contempt for me. Seems like betrayal is in the family genes; it's a part of the crooked psyche.

It stinks.

You see, nothing changes on the outside. You convince yourself as soon as you start your term that the world will stop and wait for you to come out. The world will wait for you to see the people you love, do the things you'd promised you'd do to make it up to them.

But no, the world doesn't stop: it keeps on spinning, while precious life ends.

CHAPTER 19

Back in my room, I sit on my bed. I want to scream. I want to see her smile at me as she always does. I want her to hug me like she used to when I marched out of the school gates. She'd straighten my fleece, chastise me for being such a 'godawful mess', then look at me like I was perfection.

Back then, she was the one who made me realise I could do things, I could achieve. Dad'd just see me and Harrie as something to keep the wife occupied, something to keep her out of his hair.

Mum, pushed us to do things, to listen, to be...

But now, all I want to be is on Howard wing ICU, battering their padded walls, shouting and kicking the life out of myself. But instead, I sit coiled, a gun, cocked and ready, loaded with anger, hate and primed ready to fire.

Lethal!

They're giving me a special day release to visit Mum. Dad says she's on life support, for Christ's sake. They can keep her going until I arrive to touch her cheek. She won't feel it; speak to her, she won't hear me; be there, she won't know.

I want time out. I want time out there to give back to her everything she gave to us. Time to tell her she can do it, she can live the life she wants to live. She doesn't need to stay for me and Harrie any more. Wherever she wants to go, whoever she wants to be.

I'm visiting her tomorrow.

There's a tap on my door. It's Amy.

"All right, son?" He's looking solemn, like it's his pain, his problem.

"Yes, I'm OK."

"You can tray, supper in your room tonight, if that's where you want to be? Let Penny know and she'll get canteen to send something along."

Do I really want to be sitting in this shit box waiting for my mother to die?

"No, thanks, I think I'll head for the canteen and catch up with Lewis."

"Good lad!" He says it like I've just scored a freakin goal. "Best to keep busy."

"Yes."

"Anything you need, just let me know," he says. "Well, I'll leave you to it."

Yeah, Amy, there is something I need: give me back the last three years of my life. Let my mother know that I'm there, let her hear me say, "I'm coming home soon, and I'll never let you down again. Mum – I'm sorry."

And, for the first time since I walked through the doors of HMYOI Hendbrook, I'm sobbing. The gut-wrenching, body-shaking sob that drains me of every ounce of my being.

I skipped supper. No food, no noise, no stench of canteen grease, disinfectant and body odour. I sit up through the night. I sit and wait. I wait for the knock on my door and Amy or Penny to step in and say, "You're too late, she's gone."

L. James has released me from post duties: Amy shoved the note into my pigeon-hole before heading off duty at 5 a.m.

So, I drag my carcass down to the showers, then head over for breakfast in the canteen.

Lewis is sitting talking animatedly to a kid on his wing called Ryan, and I know the conversation is running one way because Ryan's got this syndrome called Kabuki, or Kuki crap, so nobody can understand a word the poor bastard says.

Ryan seems OK with the status quo. He's grown up having the piss taken. He responds with strange, gargled noises and as long we keep on the conversation when he stops mouthing, he's happy. He just likes to be in the fray, enjoying company and we don't take the piss. For what? The guy's got a speech impediment, shit happens. He's still got a brain, for Christ's sake. Most of the inmates in this dump have got a quarter of the brain cells Ryan possesses and they talk jack shit. He's always on day release for his speech and language appointments, which is lucky; the Kabuki's not so lucky.

"Hey, here's Willy Wonka," calls Lewis as I grab a seat.

"Hi," I say, barely able to look at my food, let alone shove it down my throat.

"Hey, what's up, Willy Wonka? How'd the outing go? Any action? Bet there was some fit stuff out there. Man, I can't believe you're already on day release. I've another whole freaking year to go," he moans.

Ryan grunts an envious agreement.

"It's my mum, Lewis. She's had a stroke. She's dying." I fire it out and stare at the shitheap of mash on my tray.

We sit in silence while Lewis' sluggish brain processes the information.

"Christ! Lawrence! Sorry, mate, that's bad news, bad news." Lewis is shaking his head with Ryan nodding sombrely beside him.

"Dad came and told me last night. I wanted to tell him to shove off. He's got a bit on the side. I hate his guts," I announce.

"Did she know? Your mum, did she cotton on?" asks Lewis.

"Ahh, I'm not sure, man. She just got on with things, you know? I think so. What a shit ending, eh? What a heap of crap!" I'm shoving my food with my fork and wanting to toss it at the windows.

"Yeah, total crap," says Lewis, "but you don't want to get eaten up inside, Lawrence. There're a lot of things that go on that you can't do naff all about. And grown-ups is one of them. You can't work it out for them. Can't solve it, man."

"Yeah, but she sees me in this dump, this mess before she goes. Like, I'd planned on the out. To tell her I knew about all the stuff with Dad and it's OK. If she wanted to get out, start fresh, we'd be OK. I'd help. I can't believe it's now, man. Dad says she's out of it."

"You going to see her?" asks Lewis.

"Tomorrow."

"She'll know, man. She'll know you're there. They've done research, I read about it. Talk to her; tell her what you want to tell her. She'll hear, it's a cert. She'll hear," says Lewis, confidently.

"You really believe that?" I look across at him and Ryan, hopeful.

Lewis is pensive, certain, and Ryan's shaking in agreement like they're wise old men.

"Sure," insists Lewis. "Defo. They've done tests: brain activity, electrical impulses, it all goes up, reacts to the stimuli. Genuine, on the level. It registers when relatives visit and talk to coma patients."

Ryan nods and announces, "Dosc fanshiffooway." He works at a reassuring smile that resembles pain.

I shrug an acknowledgement, like I know Ryan's sentiment. I get the gist.

"Listen, man. Talk and she'll hear," says Lewis.

"Thanks. Thanks." Those words mean something, even if deep inside I don't believe them.

"Hey, if you want a smoke, man, a pill, or just loosen up, we can go to the gym, I'm up for it," suggests Lewis.

"Thanks. No, I'm splitting," I say.

I discard my tray full of food on the stacking trolley and wander back to my room.

I'm thinking, yeah, I can, I can say to Mum, it's OK. We'll work it all out, Mum. I'll help, anyway I can.

I spot Amar out across the quad, drifting to the canteen on the other side of the window. He catches sight of me and hurries across the yard. His hair's in a bun; it's tied on top of his head with red cloth and he's wearing outrageously striped Aladdins. I can tell, today the boy's feeling bold.

He taps the thick layers of unbreakable glass. There's no sound. But he holds his shiny fingernails up for me to admire.

I force a smile, but it's a sad one, an 'I'm trying hard but in a bad place' response.

He puts his finger to his cheek and wipes away an imaginary tear, and blows a kiss.

I put thumbs up and shrug, like, no worries, you're safe, my friend, you're safe.

We split and I carry on to my wing. All's quiet: it's lunch, everyone's out in the yard or in the canteen. But, as I go towards my room, the hairs prickle on the back of my neck. I sense someone's behind me. Yeah, the sabretooth's risen again.

There's a shadow, it's following me step by step. I get ready for trouble and when I turn, I see Walter.

"Lawrence," he says, with a cocky grin.

"Fuck off."

I step into my room and he's in, standing looking at me like he's just smelt shit and he's wearing a triumphant smirk.

"I'm out," he brags.

"Disappear. I haven't got time," I say.

He ignores me. He steps further into my room.

Bad move.

"Oh, you've got plenty of time to..." he starts, but I'm right there and I've already got him pinned by his sweaty collar to my back wall. The whites of my knuckles are pressed hard under his chubby little neck.

His eyes are bulging. "You'll gretet tis," he chokes at me.

"The only thing I regret, you little worm, is not feeding you to the crew when they asked me to. When those nobheads came to me wanting your skin I should have given it them," I hiss. "You're on your own now, Walter. There'll be a time outside when you meet me on the street and when you do – you'd better watch your back."

He's squirming in his skin and it's his fault, it's all his fucking fault, Mum, Dad, Harrie, Rich the whole shebang. It's all his fault. His face is turning purple, he's wheezing, but I keep up the pressure.

"You see, Walter, I never said a thing to that bunch of gorillas. You had a friend, man. I don't give my mates away to filth like Woods and his playmates. Oh yeah! They came for you alright and I sent them packing. They knew where I stood and it was right beside you. But, you? You're such a moron you crawled out with your slimy tail between your legs right up their arses..."

I release him and he sinks against the wall, coughing and spluttering. But when he looks at me I can tell there's recognition. There's regret; he knows I'm telling the truth. He's ballsed up big time and now he'll have to live with it for the rest of his sad days, and you know what? I want that knowledge to hurt him far more than a kick in the teeth. I want it to hurt him for good.

"Get out, you sad bastard," I hiss. "Go on, out of my sight, Walter."

CHAPTER 20

Dad wanted to come and collect me from Hendbrook and drive us both to the hospital. I said no. I put in a formal request to the Warden and it was granted. I go alone. I need to plan, to speak to Mum, if and when the time's right, and hope she'll hear me.

They've given me a forty-eight hour pass. They've booked me into the local youth hostel close to the hospital. As long as I sign in at the designated police station at the right times, I'm OK.

It's strange how the attitude towards me inside has changed. As I walk up to the hospital entrance I wonder if it's because of Gregory and my agreement to meet Rich. Or maybe it's due to L. James and his good reports. Whatever the reason, the renewed trust is one of the most important changes in my young life.

And walking up those hospital steps I'm suddenly transported back to when Mum frogmarched me up to the entrance of A & E for an X-ray and they plastered my broken arm for twelve weeks. I was eleven years old when I discovered that carrying my bike up the steps of the slide and riding it down like Eddie Crazy for a three-sixty wasn't one of the cleverest tricks I'd ever performed. However, the consequent scene of carnage and resulting war wound earned me some serious street cred. Who needs tricks when you've got a cast?

I felt a lump in my throat and tried to swallow back the emotion. That was just one of the things Mum did and I remember how young and alive she was then. And marching me through that door, she was met with so much affection.

"Jen, how's things? This is the trouble you left us for, is it?" I remember the duty doctor saying. She laughed and flirted.

A load of older nurses popped their heads round the curtain. "Let us know when trouble settles down, we're short-staffed. And you, cut out the extreme sports!" they said.

I smiled, embarrassed that I was with some celebrity.

Mum was so chuffed that the staff remembered her, had so much respect for her. She marched down the corridors like she was bringing me home.

My guts start churning at the thought of how she is now.

In the hospital it hits me: the senses, the echoes, people floating down the corridors, the rubber floors, the fire doors, the thick glass of the shatterproof windows. I am in an institution. Once you've lived in one for more than a month, you can smell them a mile off, no matter what sign's pinned to the door. The hospital lighting is brighter, but it's the same faceless building as Hendbrook, filled with people suffering from a whole different kind of sickness.

There're a load of other problems in this place.

It takes me forever to locate the IC ward or maybe I've just been wandering, trying to suspend the moment when I have to walk up to Mum's bed and see what I don't want to see. I arrive at the small nursing station and ask for Mum and the blue-jacketed male orderly nods and tuts sympathetically, then shows me to the side ward where Mum's plugged into her machinery.

I can see her white outline on the bed, which is placed at the end of the side ward under sharp, fluorescent light. I can hear the beepers, see the red lights flashing on the holder of the tubes as they empty the fluid out of the plastic bottles into her thin hand. I'm fighting back the tears. Gotta be strong. But my heart is cracking and splintering into tiny pieces. I can feel each piece cutting into my chest, forcing me to fight for breath.

She looks different; her face is now a strange, lop-sided mask. But she's also the same. She's Mum, just as she's always been. I reach out and gently stroke her hand. It's purple: bruised from where they'd put the needles in, then removed them in favour of other more accessible veins. I stroke her cool skin; it's fine, paper-thin, like tissue. I can see the blue and pink of her delicate veins.

I quietly pull up a seat.

"Hey, Mum. It's me, Lawrence. I'm here, Mum." I'm quiet, but the ward is so still, hanging static: a snapshot of a moment that seems to last forever. I sit, away from the frenetic intensity of the other wards. It's so calm.

I think of Lewis' words. But looking at her, I've lost every ounce of belief in them. The reality destroys the fantasy. Mum's locked inside somewhere far, far away. She's just lying, empty, hardly functioning at the most basic level. She's barely here. But I can't help myself; I talk to her – just in case. I hope. Oh, how I hope.

"I came up by myself today, Mum. All the way from Hendbrook, just for you. See, you're so important they let me come and visit without an escort. I got the train," I say, "the high speed. Must be on the rise because I got good references from L. James, you know the ex-army warden, the one I told you about once. He works in the post room with me. He's sound, really sound."

I sit and wait, for how long I don't know. I look for a flicker, a twitch, a slight movement. There is none.

I sit silently, defeated, and study my grubby hands. This is not working. I don't have the power to change this, to make Mum better. I can't do this.

I glance around the ward, wondering if I should just kiss her goodbye, then go. I sit, silent, inadequate, for the rest of the afternoon. Staff pop in and out, I acknowledge, move back from the machines, but they say, it's OK. I can stay just where I am. They can reach her bags and so they keep putting new ones in, one after the other and still nothing happens, but they check her stats until they say, sorry it's end of visiting and I must go.

I hop up, grateful for the prompt.

"I'll be back tomorrow," I say to the nurse.

"Fine," she says as she picks up Mum's records, tick, cross, tick, cross. Mum's just another mark on the records now, just like Yours Truly.

Nineteen hundred hours, I'm back at the police station and up to the desk to announce my arrival. There's no rush as they book me in. I'm surprised they don't expect me to do a runner. But then, I'm nearly for the out, they'll know that.

The copper nods. "Take a pew, if you don't mind." Then he's off ferreting around the back office and comes back with a printed sheet.

"Sign here."

I scribble my name. Now I'm property of HMP I have to do a lot of signing, Yours Truly.

"You're at the hostel on Park Street. Know where that is?" he asks, kind of friendly.

"No."

"You're in luck; it's just round the corner."

"Thanks."

"Back here nine a.m. tomorrow morning, please, sir," he says.

"Yes, I know."

"Right, see you then."

The room in the hostel's not too bad. The place stinks of cheap air freshener and disinfectant to which I've added my own pungent takeaway. I nibble the chips and bin the rest. I feel sick. Then I think of when I come out in a few weeks and know that Mum's not going to be there to share it, my new life. She won't celebrate, in some warped kind of way, the fact that I've done my time, faced up to my sentence and I'm starting over.

I feel a surge of anger. It's heating my cheeks; pumping round my veins until the rage overwhelms me and I reach down and punch the shit out of the chair, the bed, everything. It's selfish, it's childish, but some small part of me is angry with Mum. It's hard to believe, but I feel robbed of sharing that moment of freedom with her, with someone who actually gives a shit.

BALANCE

I collapse on the bed, exhausted, spent.

Harrie! She'll be coming to see Mum. But when? Harrie will be getting on with her life, her degree. She'll be flourishing at university, ticking all the right boxes. It's a different Harrie now. Was a time when she would have been here twenty-four hours, waiting, watching for Mum. Not any more. She tore this family apart. Problem is, when will she come back from uni? At weekends, I figure. Then there's no chance of us colliding. I wonder about Rich. It's not going to be easy. None of this. Then I make myself not think of Rich, Harrie or anyone but Mum.

Tomorrow, I pledge, I'll make a better fist of things. Tomorrow, I'll talk and talk at her and maybe, just maybe, she'll know I've come to say goodbye.

CHAPTER 21

I'm booked in for nine at the police station and then I head off to the hospital. I pass the places I know so well, the bus station where I hung about with my mates, the park, even my old school. There's a new prefab on the playground. I guess it's for the strugglers, the specials. They used to be shipped into the library for reading and I used to get irritated as hell when I couldn't get in for my dinosaur books. Happy days! I wander over, wrap my fingers around the mesh fence. When I left this school and went up to the High, I'd come back and jump the rooftop here; it was my training ground. Yeah, that prefab is every young tracer's dream.

I wonder what my mates are doing now. I know one of them took off to Australia for some kind of WFTA around the world. Another was an electrician's apprentice. The others, I can't remember what they planned, what they went on to. I never had the chance to find out. All I know is that I'm on day release from HMYOI and out of all the people in our group, this middle-class twat is the one who took a fall.

Classic!

There were plenty in my year my folks didn't want me to fraternise with: lots of dubious characters or related to parents of ill repute. And here I am, Lawrence, the fallen angel of the Respectables, out of HMP for the day.

I smirk in anger, but the shame wins. I put my head down and walk on.

It never occurred to me that I'd pass the same warehouse where it all kicked off nearly three years ago. Shit! It's still there, still empty, boarded up and awash with street art and protests in graffiti. It's prime for the next illegal rave and consequent raid. The scene of my nightmares stands here, my daymare.

I want to walk past, but I can't. I'm drawn to it, emotions pulling me along, irresistible. I wander across the road and stand looking at the black iron door and the metal steps of the fire escape, leading to the rooftop.

The crime scene.

There're still the ridiculous official warning signs: NO ENTRY, DANGER, PRIVATE PROPERTY, pinned to the doors and windows; enticing the more adventurous kids in the area to take a chance, get a hit, just as I used to.

I touch the railings that curl up the side of the building. It was here I climbed to escape Rich; it was here I clambered to the sound of pounding music inside the warehouse, kids hollering and screeching. I close my eyes but see vividly behind the lids the lights. I smell the smoke, weed, beer, vomit. It all comes back and I want to block it out. I can't.

I climb over the feeble barrier of plastic taping and ascend the grilled steps. I hear the familiar clang of my footsteps echoing as I walk. I rise, feeling the breeze build into a brisk wind buffeting against my cheeks as I step over the ladder and on to the flat rooftop.

I navigate my way around and over the roof vents and head to the edge.

I peer over.

Christ!

It's catches my breath: I can't believe Rich fell so far and survived. How would it be if I jumped, how quick? Depending. Such an efficient death if I tipped myself one way, or the other. Head first. I could make it the end in a millisecond.

What a fitting finale to a screwed-up young life. I'd die in place of Rich. Pay the price for the damage I've inflicted on his broken body, his shattered life. Die and never leave the institution and that way never be angry with Mum for not being there. Never be the failure I'm already mapped out to be for the rest of my sad life. Dad, finally he'd be relieved of his problem, he could move on with his life.

Balancing out the justice, just the way Harrie wants it to be – me, not Rich.

It all fits nicely into the jigsaw. It seems right, fair, even-stevens, yeah? This way, is the right way.

The toes of my trainers are spread across the sharp ledge. I sway. Bending forward, I gaze on to the busy road below. I'm not high on chemicals this time, I've got no one to run away from this time. It's just me, the past – and the contemplation of a shattered future.

Harrie, here's to you.

When I started my term at Hendbrook, the counselling team swooped like vultures. Depression's rife in YOIs. Kids starting their term use the opt-out clause with canteen knives, illegal drugs or sleepers from the medical store. Most offenders court trouble. They fight their way through the nightmare and soon realise no one's interested, no one gives a shit if they end up on Howard wing in a padded cell.

This option, over the edge, would be quick. If I jump off the right way, I know I can make it work fast, dead on impact. And the weird thing is – I'm not scared of dying. I've never contemplated death as anything to fear. It's just there, like a vacant room waiting for me to open the door and step through. I just need to take one more step.

Someone coughs behind me, a nervous 'I don't want to send this screwball over the edge' cough.

I turn around. There's some overweight security guard standing smiling amiably, but I can see in his eyes he's scared shitless.

"You OK, son?" he asks. "Better come away from the edge."

I hadn't planned to end my life in front of some uniform, that's for sure.

"Yes, just taking in the views," I say, with a nonchalant shrug.

"Right, not supposed to be up here. It's private property. There's a nice place in the middle of town, it's a hotel; sometimes they let you go on the roof terrace and enjoy the views," he says, like I can go and top myself someplace else, at the nice hotel?

I can see he wants to shift the responsibility, have this nasty potential off his watch.

I step back from death and walk towards life.

"Yes, thanks," I say, as I stride past.

He turns and follows me down to the street, to ensure I piss off.

I'm back out on to the main pavement. I look up. and think about Rich, about Harrie.

Yeah, I think about living.

CHAPTER 22

I get to Mum's ward around ten. I've got to be back at the police station and booked for twelve, then on the train and at Hendbrook by teatime.

I should feel grateful that they've released me for the three days visiting, a bit like compassionate leave, I guess, like when you're in the military. But today, I don't appreciate it and I think this will be the last time I see Mum and then what? Plans are screwed. I had it in my head, I was going to help her, to tell she doesn't have to live a lie for me and Harrie any more.

There's a dark pink bunch of Sweet William on the way to the hospital, perfect: they were her favourite. Were, because to me, Mum's gone now and already I see her in the past tense.

At her bedside, I wave the flowers under her piped-up nose. Then bend over and kiss her cool forehead.

"Hey, Sweet William, Mum, the really smelly ones you like." I put them on the wheelie cupboard beside her. Today she seems thinner than yesterday, if that's possible. As if her skin has been drawn tautly over her small-boned frame.

"Have to head back today, Mum. Two days they gave me and it feels more like two hours. But wanted to talk to you. See, how it's been with the old man for you, it's been tough. You must've been lonely. S'pose me and Harrie – when we were at home, it kept you busy, company, right? But we're not there any more and you need to know, even if you go, we'll always be around for you. Problem was, is, you're too clever at hiding things. Yeah, smart. But me and Harrie aren't kids any more. So, we can take the break..."

The words get stuck in my throat. I look at her and see there're no formulas that'll change what her life was when she was well, before she crashed into some place between life and death. Nothing I can say can change that. She's frozen in the back then.

The machines work away and a part of me wishes they'd stop.

I clench my jaw with the need to shout at something: at whatever's turning the world into the darker place it's become.

I sit and watch the nurses at the desk, tick, box, tick. Some green-uniformed orderly trundles noisily down onto the ward with a trolley full of packs. Like, everyone's out cold and no one's told her? The nurses keep tick, ticking while trolley walks up along the beds anyway and looks at the shut-eyes, the silent sleepers. Then, satisfied no unconscious wants tea or biccies, she rattles her kit away like she's some trolley dolly at a show.

A part of me wants to laugh, not because it's funny, but because it's so shitting unfunny.

I close my eyes and tell myself to shut the shit up in my head, and start talking to Mum.

BALANCE

"Hey, remember when you brought me here and I got plastered up? You were livid. But your old workmates came round and you were loving it and I remember you fancied that Dr. Can't remember his name. You said he was 'to die for' and I said, 'Mum, he's a doc; die on him and he'll be pretty miffed. You spoilt me for three weeks because I had so much pain from my break. Maybe the old man's right: I have been spoilt. Always been happy at home with you and Harrie. Is that being spoilt?"

I sit and watch the activities of the staff out in the main corridor. They're floating in, lifting boards at the end of the beds, reading, ticking around the ward.

Time passes.

I look back at Mum and struggle to come up with any meaningful conversation.

"I've started to write up my journal. Things like about you choosing my name and your friend who worked with you at the hospital and the comp to see who had their kid first. Bet you thought I'd forgotten about that."

Suddenly someone's standing at the end of the bed.

At first I think it's a nurse, but when I look round, I see Dad.

"Hello, son," he says.

He's standing holding a bunch of Sweet William too.

Voila!

He's dressed casual, halfway between work and play. Like he's been golfing, looking sporty for the ladies. He's darker, tanned and polished his hair up with a nice shine.

I make a move to go.

"No, don't stand up. I'll get another chair," he says.

"Gotta go. I've got to book in and get back. I'm on a timer."

"Right," he says peering down at Mum. "She's not in any pain, you know. They reassured me there's no pain. That's the main thing."

"What the hell do they know?"

He flinches in shock, then readjusts. "More than you think, son," he says, sadly.

"Yes, maybe," I concede, a little calmer. I reach out and touch Mum's cool hand.

"Want a lift to the station? I can come straight back and sit with Mum after. I didn't know you were out or I would have come and picked you up. Five minutes' drive won't..."

"No, you're OK. I'm meeting another day release and we're walking back together." I lie, again.

I kiss Mum's hand and place it carefully on to the sheet.

"Bye, Mum," I say, "love you."

I ease my way around Dad.

"Why don't you let me drive you both back then, you and your friend? It'll give you an extra half an hour to get a coke. Here," he's shoving the flowers under his arm and reaching for his wallet, like cash is the way back in.

"I'm good. Meal's already set, thanks. Got to split," I say, and I'm out of that room and down the corridor.

I'm gone.

The ride back's not so bad. I sit and look out of the window. Maybe it's not hit me yet, not fully.

But then again, maybe it's because I've seen Mum, spent some quiet time with her, told her I loved her and if, but I don't believe it'll happen, if she starts living again, things can be different. I feel kind of more at peace inside. Sad as hell, but calmer. I think I can forgive her. I think it's OK to let her go.

I guess I wouldn't have jumped off that rooftop. I smile: good call.

In fact, I look like a weirdo, 'cause I'm sitting beaming at my reflection in the window when I know, no shitting way would I have jumped off that rooftop.

CHAPTER 23

"Morning, Lawrence." L. James is bagging up in the post room.

"Morning, sir," I say. In a strange way there's comfort in this mindlessly boring task.

"Do me a job will you?" he says, and I'm surprised he's not barked it at me as an order like he usually does. It sounds more like a workmate's request.

"Go and get me coffee, a good strong one, not the decaf shit from the machine, white with sugar. I need the sugar. The wife had her hip replaced yesterday and they shipped her straight back home. Don't even keep them in for the night. More like a bloody spare parts service than a hospital. I've been up all night." He's digging into his pocket for the change.

"No, that's OK. sir, I can get this," I say.

"Nice of you, Lawrence, but we can't accept things from those serving," he says politely.

"A big bribe! A coffee, sir, and your career's done," I say, raising my brow in false horror. "We could both go down for a long time for this."

He laughs. "OK, smart arse, coffee's on you."

BALANCE

I'm back with the heat of the paper cup searing into my fingertips.

"Thanks," he says. L. James drinks the molten lava straight down and I stand and watch with deep respect.

"I wouldn't bloody well mind them sending the wife back home if they'd let me sleep in her bed in hospital. I've been shunted to the spare room and that bed's not been used since the lad left home," he moans.

My ears prick up. This is another side to L. James that's pretty interesting and it kills the boredom of weighing browns all day.

"What's he doing? Your son." I suddenly see L. James as a different kind of animal. He's a family man, normal with kids or a kid at least. Always thought of him as coming out of the woodwork here to torment the offenders for the duration, then doing a vanishing act until morning. But not so! See, it's weird how perspectives change and the world for me shifts on its axis slightly.

"He's doing what his old man did, joined the forces. He's in Afghanistan, been out there for three months now," he says proudly.

"Tough call of duty, sir."

"Not for my boy. He's made of solid stuff. He's loving it."

So, I'm wondering, how anyone can love being out in a furnace full of Brit-haters, planting mines and taking pot shots at uniforms? Guess I'm just not made of that solid stuff.

Work's finished, so it's time to head back to my room before going to the canteen. As I pass Walter's door a new resident glances nervously out at me.

Crime rate must be on the rise. The kid looks to be fourteen, maybe fifteen years old. He's sitting on Walter's bed and he's crying. Poor sod's just the same age as I was when I first came in.

I linger, then head on.

It's tough when you're first banged up, for sure.

I think of Walter, waive the action, then decide; two Walters in one stint would be the worst luck in the world. So, I come back out and tap on his door.

"Hey, man, meet the neighbour, on this side."

I smile, but it's not getting through.

He looks up: scared and angry all in one glance.

"I'm going to the canteen. The food's shit – but it fills a hole," I say. "You can pace down with me."

He looks at his tatty trainers and thinks and sniffs and thinks some more.

He's blacker than Amar. I guess he's from the Caribbean or his folks were. He's got a nose stud that glints when he moves his head. It looks cool, the kind of cool that I can't wear; some aren't built for that style.

He stands slowly and tugs on his joggers, like to tidy what? Then he shuffles silently out.

As we walk, I can see him looking at the other prisoners, his eyes shifting side to side, as if ready to flee. Problem is, in this place, there's nowhere to run.

Time to lighten the air.

"Time flies, man, in here. It just shoots past like a rocket," I lie, "but you've got to keep busy, keep moving. Do things, get involved, you know? If you don't – you get cabin fever and..."

He just listens and that's OK. He's not mouthy, not proud of his record like some of them or angry enough to try and beat the shit out of the wardens or other offenders.

Lewis is sitting at the tables talking to Andy from our wing. Lewis looks at me and studies the newbie with interest.

We gravitate to the trays, slam spoonfuls of colour on our plates, then head across to sit beside them.

"Hello, gentlemen," says Lewis. "How you doing, Lawrence? Did you talk to your mum?"

My visit to Mum seems like a lifetime ago instead of only yesterday. It's amazing how quickly a body readjusts to being back inside, almost like never out.

"Yes, I talked, but I know she didn't hear. It's OK. I got to see her, Lewis, that meant a lot, mate," I said.

"Commiserations, man," says Andy, flicking back his long blond fringe.

"Yes, thanks."

The newbie takes a seat.

I gesture. "This is my new neighbour." I turn to him. "Don't know your label, man."

"It's George, but people call me, G," says George quietly. Then he hammers in forkfuls, panic-struck, like someone's going to do a snatch and grab.

"Great, then I'm an A," says Andy.

"I'm Lawrence. But you can call me Lawrence," I say.

The corner of G's mouth twitches. He's not sure, yet. He's all coiled up.

"Hey, man, I was just telling Lewis – here the worst thing about being inside is no sex," announces Andy. "Outside, man, I was doing it every night. Had a couple of lookers on the go and I'd had a good rota set, real professional, one bird Monday to Weds, the next, Thurs to Sat. Sunday was my day of rest." Andy laughs.

"No shit!" I exclaim with false surprise. "That's some action. Must be your irresistible animal smell, Andy."

"Oh, I got it all right," he says, not picking up the jibe. "Hell, it's tough. But I've got some good pics, fit ones to delight the senses, fire up the furnace, man," offers Andy.

Lewis is sniggering next to me. I'm keeping my face straight as a line.

"Masturbation's good for the soul," announces Lewis.

I look at him and grin.

He shrugs, lifts his arms, all puzzled, "What? It's a fact. I read it. Where was it? Oh yeah, that Jehovah's Witness rag they shoved in my pigeon-hole. Yep, straight up."

" 'No kidding, I'm in the wrong church, man," says Andy.

Now I can see George is smiling back the pasta.

"They've got meetings, time's on the board, Friday nights, in the old gym. Get over there, man. They bring in special weeklies, I've seen them. Learn to play your organ, and boy, the girl who plays it!" says Lewis, making a big boob gesture.

"A fit girl? I'm over there," says Andy as he stands and grabs his empty tray. "Yes, it's torture man, torture. Nowhere can a dude get a decent shag round here. See ya. Jahovers, here I come."

Lewis spits out his food and snorts as Andy disappears.

I shake my head in despair.

"The guy's a virgin," Lewis declares.

I smile. "Yeah!"

And G's lips are wide.

G's hungry. He wolfs down the tray full of baked spuds and beans and his eyes are darting round, he's hunting for more. That's something different about us, G and me. I couldn't eat for a week when I was first banged up. Although it could be the last of G's drugs wearing off that's pushing him to fill his tanks.

But I remember the wardens got a tad concerned, thought I was hunger-striking for a while.

"How's it going?" I ask Lewis.

Lewis beams. "Tell you what, my friend, when I'm out you're doing my laundry for me, as arranged, and we shall eat like kings, indeedy."

"Wash your soils? You'll be lucky, dweeb. So you're planning to take a room in Buckingham Palace?"

"Nah, better than that," he says like my comment's actually serious. "I'm sous chef." Lewis rubs his shirt like he's wearing a medal. "I joined the course this week and Fra lien Frits in the kitchen? She thinks I rock, man, I actually rock."

"Hey, smart move, the kitchens," I say.

We look at G, but he's got his eyes down staring desperately at his empty tray. Like, where's the food gone? He's coming off something, for sure.

"You can ask for more, man," says Lewis. "Don't ask? You don't get. That's the deal in this kennel."

G glances around the canteen. He's jumpy, wide-eyed like an animal about to bolt.

He tenses, getting the courage to shift, then slides down the bench, stands up and goes for it.

It kind of reminds me of the film my old school took us to see in English Lit or maybe it was drama. The Victorian one about the street kid asking for more; yep, G's a regular Oliver.

"Walter shithead's gone then," says Lewis. "Just as frickin well. Apparently he had some kid done over on my wing the week he was leaving. Seems the kid looked at Wanker Walter the wrong way."

"Crazy, man, just crazy." I shake my head.

"He'll be back," affirms Lewis. "He's turned nasty, that one. The ones that are scared are the most dangerous and he's scared shitless."

"Well, you tip one way or other on those scales, man," I say.

"Right. He'd break the freekin scales if he stood on them," says Lewis with a snicker.

But I'm already somewhere else: I'm thinking I've got my meeting tomorrow with Rich. It's looming, the day I'm dreading. But I'll do it and the reason why is lying in a hospital bed.

CHAPTER 24

It's three-thirty in the morning and G is bashing his door down. He's screaming like some psycho, "Let me out, you bastards, let me out."

I try shouting above the ruckus, "G, for Christ's sake, man, cool it. Cool it."

But he's not having any of it. He's cracked big time. I know the medics will be down here pronto. I struggle out of bed under the watch light and peer out of my porthole. There's not a lot I can see, just blue uniforms, arms, legs, blue flashes. But I can hear G, he's throwing furniture around. It's hammering and crashing against the other side of my freakin wall and next time we connect up, he'll know I'm seriously pissed.

Give the uniforms their due, they try and talk to him. They keep their voices low, steady. It's a gear the blues kick into when they've got to use it. Sometimes it works, but this time, it's a no-goer.

G's lost the plot. He's in a frenzy. So finally they go in and when they do get to jacket him, he's screaming all the way up the corridor to Howard wing.

I rub my eyes and a sigh comes from nowhere. Like, I'm sorry for him, but then again I don't know what he's done. He could have knifed some poor kid. He could have wiped out some pensioner. Basically, G could be a cruel bastard: the next Petal in training. And that brings all kinds of unpleasant memories to the fore. I've learnt that you never know in this place; best to watch and wait until you've sifted the good from the bad.

I sit back on my bed and curse the shit out of him for waking me up and making me go through the long night before my meeting with Rich. Then everything settles down. I hear doors slamming. The warden's back in G's room, lights off, locked down and it's exquisitely silent once more.

I must have fallen asleep somewhere between the screaming and dawn. The keys rattle in my door and Amy's standing there. His face is lined, he looks exhausted and one hell of an upset. Yes, he's looking more tired than me. I reckon with G's little breakdown, he's had one hell of a long night shift.

"Sorry, Lawrence. I've got some bad news, lad," he says.

I know it's Mum. But I brace myself all the same. Preparing for the fact that she's finally gone.

I sit up, straight, rigid. My heart's pumping fast and I'm awake, like I've slept all the short night.

"It's Amar. He's dead," he says.

I look at him like he's wrong, like he doesn't know what the shit he's talking about.

"We lost him, Lawrence," he repeats, louder, sharper.

"Amar?"

"Sorry, son. We lost him."

I sit, rocked, disorientated, staring at him like he's crazy.

No, see, that's not how it's supposed to work, my addled brain protests. It was just a silly little game Amar played, man. It doesn't work like that.

"Lawrence – he fell unconscious last night and, Christ, well you know we had to move the new kid, George, on to the observation wing. I don't know what Amar took in, he was diabetic, you know. The lad must have loaded on Christ knows what. By the time we checked him in the medical wing, he'd already gone," Amy explains and I can tell he's gutted. He's rubbing his forehead and eyes, trying to contain the exhaustion, the sadness. He's in pieces and if he could come in and talk about it with me, he would, I can see it in his face. But he's professional, detached.

I sit, my hands clasped together, and feel my throat drying up. I stare at my desk and think letters, letters everywhere. Random thoughts float into my head, nonsense, pink blooms, Walter's beanie, Mum's Sweet William and Amar's nail varnish. What a fucking mess, my head, I can't sort out the mess in my head. Amar's gone. It's hurting somewhere in my brain, in my body, in my soul.

Maybe it's because Amar put a value on me. He rated me and yeah, I rated him. The walls stare back at me and I'm hopeless. Then it comes. I kick the chair across the room, pissed because the world has lost a unique guy, a dynamic, amazing, human being. The world's a darker place.

Amar's gone.

When did Amy go? He must have gone out of my room hours ago and I missed those hours ticking me on to my first meeting with Gregory and Rich. It's Penny's knock and the prompt, 'Get your arse over to the main offices,' that sends the spark that revs me up.

At some time during that long morning I kept floating back up to Amar's room. His door was locked, taped across as if a murder scene. But the shutter remained open and when I peered in, I saw his freakin candles and it made my gut churn.

There're hushed rumours about an enquiry. Shit! Maybe poor Amy's for the chop if they think he hasn't done his watch properly. No wonder he was so ashen. It's not just losing Amar, no, Amar was popular with the wardens despite him tormenting them. Maybe Amy knows he's failed big time. He was caught off guard, literally, and he's shaken up.

See, it's like this. Now, when I walk down the corridors, something's missing, a light's gone out, I'm cast into the shadows. I'm grieving.

I also realise that Mum's still alive. I don't know how to feel about that. There's alive and there's alive.

I'm feeling sick, the heavy nausea kind that makes me want to turn around, run and lock myself away in the safety of my cell. Yeah, the cage becomes a bolthole, a concrete cover to hide behind. Screwy thoughts, but as I walk across the green towards the offices and my first meeting with Rich, I'm going to get a whole lot more screwed.

Outside the door to the meeting room with the warden, he's already knocked once and there was no response.

I'm thinking about turning around and getting the hell out of here when Gregory opens the door.

"Ah, Lawrence, come on in," he says like an old friend.

BALANCE

I draw in a long deep breath and stand for a moment straining, unable to see Rich. Is he here yet, is he waiting?

He's not behind or around the main office, waiting to come in. I step inside and freeze. Rich is sitting just off to one side.

My body seizes up.

"There's a seat over here, Lawrence," says Gregory.

But Rich is just sitting, staring up at me. I can't read his face; I can't see what he's thinking. He's aged. He looks nearly as old as Dad. His face is lined and fatter, much, much fatter. He's not the good-looking, lean machine he used to be, that's for sure.

Gregory prompts me again towards a leather chair at the end of the coffee table.

I'm kind of lost. I haven't said a word. I'm mute. My head's empty, yet full of thoughts careering around, colliding like bolts of electricity sparking through my brain, I'm short-circuiting and I can't stop. My eyes are gazing at the door. It's shut, there's no out.

I sit down and it's silent. But Rich is eyeing me up, like he's trying to read me too. My hands are sweating. I don't know if I can hack this. I want to run away, escape. My clothes tighten as I squirm inside my heavy tee and joggers.

Gregory is writing a hundred to the dozen and I'm there like some condemned man facing the person I almost wiped out. Amar's face comes and fades in my mind. I look down at my trainers and clutch the end of my seat.

Then from somewhere, as Gregory scribbles away I look from the wall to the floor, to the table and then at Rich. He's gripping his chair too, and it occurs to me that maybe he's feeling more screwed-up, more scared than me.

"Rich," I say quietly.

"Hello, Lawrence," His voice is heavy, different.

"Good, right," says Gregory, briskly discarding the pen and notes on to the coffee table. "Firstly, I have to say to both of you that it's a courageous move, particularly for you, Richard, to come here and open a dialogue with Lawrence. But as I explained when we met last week, the healing process is far more successful when victims do this. And Lawrence, it's hard, I know, but you're going to find it'll get easier."

Silence. Gregory waits, for what I don't know. Maybe he's giving us space to respond. He seems to be good at that, just sitting and waiting.

Rich is still looking at me, like he's trying to see through my skin, see what's happening inside. I stiffen up; I feel exposed, no armour.

"You might think," Gregory continues after a while, "that you have nothing to say to one another. That's natural. But often, once the dialogue begins it opens the floodgates and well, then you're both on your way. It gets easier."

Rich nods. I keep looking over at him, but when our eyes engage, I look down. I'm ashamed. Sad for Amar. I can't figure what's going on inside. I keep looking at the door, desperate.

"You're looking well, Lawrence," says Rich.

"Thanks." I don't deserve the thought, not one ounce of interest from Rich.

I bite my lip as I struggle to get my brain functioning, searching for the right words to throw across the dark chasm between me and Rich.

BALANCE

"How are you?" As soon as I've asked the question I know it's a massive blunder. It's trite, feeble.

He smirks, the anger at me.

I wish I hadn't opened my mouth – stupid.

But I'm facing my past, what I've done.

"They're pleased with my progress. Still can't digest steak. I really miss the steak," he says. "But I can eat more than I could a year ago, let's say? So long as most of it's blended, you know, like baby food so you can't differentiate one flavour from the other."

"Right, tough." I look back down and think that's bad news.

"You eat steak, Lawrence?" Rich demands.

My eyes widen at the sharpness of his question.

"Kind of, when they serve it up in the canteen," I say, grinding my jaw with the guilt.

Rich nods. "Canteen food, eh?" he says cynically.

I agree.

"I meant to ask, does anyone want a coffee, tea?" asks Gregory.

"No, thanks," says Rich and I confirm.

"Right, fine. So, Rich, you mentioned to me that you'd like to talk directly to Lawrence about things, possibly the night it happened?" asks Gregory.

I'm clutching that chair tighter now and tensing my body. I can't bolt; I must stay – must listen.

"Do you remember, Lawrence?" says Rich.

I shake my head. "Not much. I can't remember much."

"Probably because you were off your stupid little head," snaps Rich.

I look across at Gregory, hoping he'll let me out, but he's intently ignoring me, focusing on nothing on a page.

I deserve the disgust and contempt tossed at me.

"No stress, Lawrence," assures Rich. "Memories are not why I'm here. I've got no interest those," says Rich. "None of us want that. It's about today, tomorrow. That's why I'm here."

My shoulders slouch with relief.

But we're both sitting, silently drawn back down into the bleak horror of that night.

I can still feel the metal rails in my hands and hear Rich shouting and he's snapping at my heels as I climb the ladder on to the warehouse roof.

The thin tin roof is throbbing from the beat of music beneath.

"Hey, watch this trick." My voice is coming down a tunnel in echoes and it's mingling with shouts and wild laughter below. I'm spinning around, my arms outstretched. I do a handstand on the roof. Here I am, get a load of this. Ectasy is surging through my body.

But Rich the Righteous is coming, he's transformed; it's cartoon capers coming right at me.

Level 2.

Something's dragging me along, man.

He's talking at me, talk, talk, talk and I'm laughing, I want to hug the big guy.

"Come on, Rich," I say, reaching out. "We're good me and you, big bro. I love you, man."

BALANCE

But now he's shouting and dragging me along. I can feel him grabbing my fleece. I shove him off. "Hey, Rich, stop, man. Come on! You and Harrie, come and meet the friends," I call.

I feel a jab, a sharp pain on my chin.

Christ! He's tried to floor me. I stand up. "What the fuck?" I'm shouting, "Get off my case!" Hey, it's cool, I'm liking everyone. "You're my best mate, Rich, we're safe," I say. "Come on."

"I'm not telling you again, Lawrence. I'm not talking any more. Last chance to get down those steps," but he's singing at me, I can tell, this guy's not really angry. I'm grinning, full of happiness. I've got a warm feeling in my belly. The world is beautiful. "Look at the stars, Rich. Plasma, glowing, living."

But Rich's mouth is moving fast forward. "Down, down, down, down," cartoon Rich is saying. He's slapped me hard on the cheek. Yeah, I can feel the burn. I step back, hands up. "Cut it out, come on." I don't want to strike back. No way, I'm not striking back.

But he's lost it. "I'm not asking you, Lawrence. I'm telling you." He's shouting now and the words jumble up with her voice: it's Harrie. She's here.

I can taste my blood from my lip trickling into my tongue.

"Rich, don't let him fall," I hear her voice, ringing in with the music.

He comes at me again. This time, he grabs my shoulder.

I reach out with my palm and shove him away. But he's gripping, vice-like. I grab his fingers and prise them off.

167

"Piss off," I shout. Now I want to cry. "Why are you being such a freakin asshole, Rich?"

He's shouting too. He raises his fist and I duck. Then... Cartoon man is gone. He's disappeared. No lives left. Game over.

I remember now, standing, the wind blasting screams into my head, cutting up the night. I remember, one minute he was there, the next.

Me and Rich, I realise, we're both sitting, mute, chaotic, crushing images shooting through our heads.

Gregory breaks the agony.

"We don't have to continue, if you don't want to, Richard. We can do this in short sessions. Even if it takes six, ten or longer, sessions, that's fine – whatever works." Gregory's holding out a get out of jail card to him and he's not taking it? I'm looking, my eyes pleading for him to take it.

"We're not going to need another meeting," announces Rich. His voice has altered into certainty; he's back in control. I'm not. I'm free-falling.

"Oh!" Gregory exclaims. He fiddles with his pen, clicking it in his hand, weighing up the situation. I'm looking at the clicker and wanting to break it into pieces.

"No, but thanks, Mr Gregory... I think I'd like to speak to Lawrence alone, though. Just me and him, if you don't mind," says Rich.

"We don't normally encourage unsupervised contact, not on the first meeting," asserts Gregory.

I look across. Rich is sure. He's gazing back, his eyes are full of intent and I know I have to do this. I go for it.

"I'm happy to speak alone too, sir, if he's OK with that."

Gregory's relaxed expression has gone. He's frowning, the clicking's stopped and his pen is poised in the air. He's fazed: he's not sure how to proceed.

"You assured me this would be led by me," insists Rich to Gregory.

"Of course, but... it's not normal procedure. For either party. It takes time."

"Time? We don't have," asserts Rich, "I'm requesting we go forward alone. Please don't worry, I don't have a loaded weapon at the end of my walking stick," says Rich.

Nice one! The bitterness bites me right where it hurts most.

Gregory purses his lips. Then after consideration he stands up, stacks the papers into his folder and slips it under his arm.

"You both have ten minutes. Sorry, I can't allow any longer unsupervised on a first meeting. The security guard is outside. If you need..."

"I know, we'll be OK. Won't we, Lawrence?" says Rich.

"Yes."

Gregory's out.

"Lawrence – I don't want to go through this again. So let's get this done," says Rich.

"I can do that. Whatever you want," I say. My foot's twitching, I'm ready to bolt.

"Does it shock you to see me like this?" he asks.

I look at him in surprise. OK, he's looking ancient, tired, yeah, different. I glance up and down in confusion.

"I don't think you look much different," I lie, again and again.

He stands up and leans on his chair. He's wobbling, looking like he's going to take a tumble. He's lopsided, shaking and swaying. Christ! Like he's geriatric. I move forward reaching out to support him, but he puts his hand up and I retreat.

He unbuttons his shirt and pulls it open.

A scar runs from his neck right down to his crotch.

"Jesus!" He's a mess.

He buttons his shirt back up, grabs his walking stick and hobbles to the sofa like some old man. He's in pain and he collapses down close to where I'm seated.

He leans forward and drops the stick.

I go to pick it up.

"Leave it," he snaps and glares.

"Rich," I start, but nothing follows. There's nothing because I can't find the words. I can't think of anything powerful enough to make it right.

Not because I wouldn't mean it, but it's done, the irreversible sentence.

"You're near the end of your term," he says. "I've been counting, counting the days you've been in."

"Yes," I say. I had wondered, sometimes, if Rich would be on the out, thinking of my time, thinking of my life.

"What are you going to do, Lawrence? What are you going to do with the rest of your life? Not that I really give a shit if you're happy or not."

"I don't know, man. I don't know."

He smirks. "One day, you'll be OK. You'll have a lovely wife, kids..." His voice begins to tremble, his eyes, they're misting up. And I know he's thinking of Harrie.

BALANCE

"Please man ..." I clench my fists and hope he doesn't cry, no, don't cry on me, Rich, anything but that.

But it's too late, he's got a tissue out, he's rubbing his eyes and holding it there, gripping the white paper as he draws in a long deep breath.

I wait. I think of the guy I worshipped. I think of Harrie's boyfriend, the cool rower, the handsome, dynamic and committed teacher. The guy who engaged with me, took an interest, became someone special in our lives. He cared.

"Don't get this wrong, I'm not crying because of you, Lawrence. It's Harrie, not you. I swore I wouldn't ..."

Her name cuts through my skin, making my blood heat up, my face burn and I know it's not working. This plan's not working.

He's bracing himself as he looks over at me. "One day you'll be cruising through life," he says, fighting to stay in control. "All this will be a thing of the past, a distant memory. You'll see yourself as someone else. That kid who did what you did, he'll be gone. Three years, three years is nothing. This is my life, now. I'm going to tell you the times I wanted to appeal, to petition for you to be sent down for a long, long time, but it was Harrie." He waits while he fights to regain his composure.

I look at him in surprise, yet I know I shouldn't be. "I don't know what I'll be doing, Rich. It's all pretty fucked up," I say.

He looks back with contempt. "I know, because you're young. You'll get over this little blip in your life. It's not left you crippled and scarred like me." His eyes are darkening with anger.

I look away from the rage. "No, right now, I don't know," I say.

"I do. Your scars will fade, mine won't. But, there's something I need you to do."

I turn back, wanting to bring both our agonies to an end. "Anything, man. Just ask," I say.

"I want you to look out for Harrie. She needs you."

I clench my fists: I'm being asked the impossible.

He shakes his head. "Harrie. It wasn't her fault. I was the fool who went up to try and get your stupid ass down that night. And since, the nights and days I lay cursing, wishing to God I'd left you to fall off that rooftop, Lawrence. I've longed for it to be you."

I brace myself against his fury, sit up straight, steady.

He stops, draws in breath as I wait for more pain to hit me. But somehow, I want to reach out and break through the rage, because I see the old Rich. The guy I worshipped.

I don't have the courage, I'm spineless and he's broken.

I watch and wonder how long has he been waiting to see me. How many days and nights has he rehearsed these lines?

His eyes are streaming. He's wiping them and looking right at me and I see what he's enduring.

"Rich, I ... There's no way. Harrie, me, it'll all be good, man. I swear. I know you love her. Listen, man, I never meant for ..."

Rich is shaking his head, trying to get it all in order.

"I swear, I know what you did for me and Harrie."

He wipes his eyes and rests his head back in exhaustion.

"Harrie, she needs you. Don't fuck her life up too, Lawrence. Out of all of us, she stands a chance, a chance to heal and she deserves it. You were her life and now that I'm gone," he says and he looks at me, accusing.

I'm squirming, writhing. Looking at the door, the floor, the door. Trying to lie, I have to lie, but this is not the deal. My whole shitty little existence has been built on lies. But I can't make this deal. Harrie's history.

"You see, Lawrence, I've let her go," he says quietly. "Harrie needs something from you, you've got to let her move forward." He's waiting, holding out for the pledge and I have to do it, I have to lie. I have to say, yes.

"Rich, inside here or out, it's me and it's you. Nothing's going to change that, man," I swear.

"It's Harrie," he insists, hammering his stick down. "Your own fucking sister."

I raise my hand and shake my head in acceptance. "Yes, I know. I hear you, Rich."

I sit while he waits for me to say what he can really believe. I have to do this. I have to add to the layers of lies.

"Me, Harrie. It'll be good between us. It'll be good."

I say it like it's a truth, like it's not churning me up to deceive the guy I almost destroyed.

We sit silently together, connected by our past, fighting to map out the crooked lines to some kind of future. There's a tentative knock on the door.

Gregory's back in.

"Oh!" he exclaims, finding Rich sitting opposite me on the sofa.

"Sorry, time up," says Gregory.

"It's fine. Lawrence was just on his way out," says Rich.

I stand up and feel a rush of blood to the head. I'm swaying, unsteady. I feel like I've just been kicked in the gut.

Rich leans down, scratches around for his stick, then bravely hauls his contorted body up from the sofa.

He reaches out to shake my hand, but I step up and lock my right arm around his.

"Rich," I say, and grief washes over me. All the sadness sweeps through my body as I think of Rich, Amar, life.

I gulp back the pain and feel my eyes burning. "Thanks for seeing me."

He nods.

"Take care, Lawrence – of you and Harrie," he says.

As I walk back down the corridor to my wing, I feel as if a door to the past is closing, ready to be bolted behind me. I'm locked deeper in because of Rich.

I won't be going back. Harrie's done. I'm done.

I see another door opening; it's the one I'm forced to take.

I can't give Rich what he needs, not now, not ever. I will live a life of deceit.

CHAPTER 25

G's back on the wing. He's reinstalled in his room, but he's not connecting with me. He's shut down. And frankly, after Amar? I don't give a toss.

If he hadn't been such a pain in the arse and distracted the night watch, Amar would still be alive. Massive miscalculation. Amar knew it was a gamble, but it was something I'd never believed he'd lose.

So, G's back. I would, if I were staying on, do something, say something, who knows? But I'm not and so it's down to him, to G, to get his head sorted. It's the only way to survive, like John Donne wrote, 'No man is an island" and it's tough enough being removed from society, let alone putting your sad ass in solitary. Maybe it's for the best that he stays clear. He gets the message, I'm pissed with him. The boy needs to source others who'll see him through his term. Then again, maybe he doesn't deserve friendship. Who knows? A lot of the kids in here are animals, no social empathy in their bones, man. They've been feral all their lives. Parents drop and dump.

Me? I've got no excuses.

But the fog's beginning to clear. I kind of get how I got here.

I thought life was a game. One big game, a laugh a minute and I played it every day.

But it's not. Life is dangerous, perilous. I have to make choices, just like the guys in that English Lit book I struggled through in class, *Enduring Love*. I've got to choose whether I grab those ropes and commit, or I turn away. Whichever way I go, I now know that choice will determine what kind of human being I am.

And – there are so many choices! It does my freakin head in.

Three days after Amar's shipped out, there's a memorial service in the chapel for him. I go with Lewis and Ryan. The chapel's pretty full, but it's mainly staff. There're just a handful of offenders and most of us are from Amar's wing.

The chaplain says the usual stuff; how Amar endeavoured to change, to make amends and was reassessing his past and looking to the future. It came over more as a preaching to the living than a tribute to the dead.

Amar's eccentric, wicked, distinct character is nowhere in the words he's spewing out across the hall. This service could be for any one of us. I bite my lip and resist the temptation to walk out in protest. I feel angry for Amar; he's been cheated out of being himself even in death: gay, flamboyant, outrageous, human.

The chaplain probably pulls out the same old tired sheet of diatribe, service after service, remembrance after remembrance. Yeah! That figures.

BALANCE

But the herd plough through it, chewing the cud and when we hit hymn number twenty-six, Abide with me, I don't even bother mouthing the words. Man! That says it all.

I'm thinking about funerals, about all the shit that goes with them and I'm thinking about Mum and feel that dull throb, that ache, right in the middle of my chest.

As we file out, I see Pevensey at the back. I knew she was there, she was singing hymns like a mad diva.

I stop beside her.

"Hello, Lawrence. So sad about our Amar," she says. "He was an odd bod, wasn't he? Was a male model, you know."

"Yes, so I heard."

Lewis is hovering. He's keen to split and hang around in the exercise area. The serious stuff just isn't his scene, he takes life as it comes – and goes.

She squeezes my arm. "You're going to miss him."

I smile. "He was a class act."

But there's also a question that I've been burning to ask since Amar died.

"Just wondering," I say to her, "a question."

"Go on, try me." She winks.

"What was he in for? Amar, what was he down for?"

I need to know in order to slot the final piece of his picture together, reassure myself that I'd guessed him right, knew him for the real person he was.

She chuckled. "Lawrence! You know I can't tell you that; I'll get a slapping down, it's confidential. I wouldn't discuss you with any of the other inmates in here."

I shrug. "I guess not."

I make a move to go, but she grabs my arm and leans closer in. "Tell you what," she says.

I wait, attentive, expectant.

She smiles. "His mum's alive and kicking somewhere in North London from all accounts. That answer your question?"

I grin. "Yes, it does, thanks. Thanks."

As the afternoon wears on, I can see that Lewis' mood is dipping, fast. He's trying not to, but he's walking heavy in the knowledge that I'm coming to the end of my term.

I'm chatting on about stuff and Lewis is nodding, but he's got this distant look in his eyes and he's not enthusiastic about the afternoon we've been given off from duties, due to Amar's service.

He's tossing a ball at his cell wall, back forth, back forth. He's been doing it for fifteen minutes while I've been filling the space.

I reach out and grab the shitting thing on its bounce.

"Balls," he says, jumping up and looking out of his window.

"Yep, if you don't cut the tossing, yours'll be aching from my trainer."

"Just try it, nob," he says. "And don't forget my list. Can't get that shit in the tuck shop here."

"There's carriage, and duty costs, man. It'll be expensive. I add on VAT."

"Vodka and tonic's good for me," he says.

"Yeah? You'll have to do more than cook for Fra Lien," I say.

He sniggers.

BALANCE

I know he'll be OK. And when he's out, I just need to keep him away from motors or maybe, I'm hoping, he's all speeded out.

CHAPTER 26

So, life's a shit. I've got five days to go to release and I'm staring at those letters from Harrie. I'm wondering, after meeting with Rich, should I open them? Can I face it all and come to terms with what she did to me?

No.

Now I'm nearing out, they let me use the IT room whenever I want, so I head up and I'm ordering flowers for Mum. I want her to have some fresh scents by her bedside. Whether she can smell them or not isn't the point. Maybe one day she'll open her eyes, even just for a moment and see them there, smell the perfume. I'd always thought I'd put them into her open hands when I knocked on the front door, a free man, like I was some returning war hero.

I close my eyes to block out the picture of how she is, where's she's lying, but they're coming from the inside, not out. I hammer the thoughts down; kill them dead by clicking the buy button. If I focus on Mum, Amar, the futility of it all, I'll end up smashing the computers and wrecking the place, just like G. No, I hold it together as I hammer my numbers in and on to order confirmation.

BALANCE

Dad's left a few messages offering to collect me from the station and drive me to wherever I need to go. Never thought he'd connect. No thanks, old man. I don't want anything but a clean break. I'll make my own way.

They keep trying to get me to make career choices. I reckon they've sold them the old story Mum used to repeat from her church when she came back and found me lolling in front of the screen: "Lawrence! The devil makes work for idle hands."

"Yeah, Mum, more fun working for him than the other guy. Anyway, my hands aren't idle, see?" I used to torment as I hammered on the joystick.

But I'm pleased to see Lewis is keeping busy these days, yeah, it's great.

He's taken to cooking like a duck to water; so much so, that when Woods came into the exercise yard and called Lewis a faggot with a spachoola, Lewis responded by giving Woods a crooked nose to go with his crooked teeth. Best day of the week, that one.

I saw Walter, yesterday afternoon tippy-tappying down the path to exit the main gates. He'd obviously been in to visit some losers in the crew, probably brought some shit in. Risky! I'm sure of something else too, Walter's still going to be broke. Joker!

The social's got me digs. It's probably a shabby little hole in town, but I'm not going home. Being there with just Dad is not an option. Not that I've had an official invitation and anyway, I don't think he hangs out there any more. I guess he's with his latest. Dad must have decided that having me

181

too close, in the vicinity, was a no-go too; it's been a subject left to fade away.

Anyway, home would be different without Mum there. I try not to think of Harrie, but then that question always hits me in the gut.

Why?

Amy's given me a batch of slips so I can sail up to Lewis' wing whenever I want and chill out with him. It's the trust. It's like gold, man. It's a whole new experience, coming up to your out. The place looks different, more open, accessible and yet it's the same terrifying prison I entered three years ago. See, it's about what's in your head, shifting perspectives.

It's a fact, since I connected with Rich: I've slept better. I still wake in the night, still have flashbacks and open my eyes in a cold sweat. But it's not so intense. I toss, turn over and go back to sleep. Never did that before. Those terrors got me up, made me run inside my cell to escape. But wondering if a different room on the outside, open free, maybe they'll stop forever.

...

Last morning and I've cruised by Ryan and the others and said my cheerios. The Vian's not been the same since Amar. I think, in fact I now know, he had a thing about Amar. Yeah, it's weird, but I got that guy all wrong. I smile, and wonder if Amar knew and what the hell must have gone through his mind.

The Vian lopes up, reaches out his long, clumsy arms and give a farewell hug, like we're best buddies and I'm genuinely touched. "Be safe, bro," he says.

"Yeah."

Then I connect up with Lewis. He's in the rec room watching some cookery programme on the morning show, but his face is blank. He's staring through the screen at the wall.

I tap him on the shoulder and he's up and downbeat, but trying to be up.

"Ready, yeah?" he says. "Packed your rubbers, man?"

I grin.

"Gloves, dickweed, for the shit you'll be shovelling."

We head over to the exercise yard and watch the eager beavers knock themselves up while we sit and chomp on the last of Lewis' chocolate bars.

"You know what? I need you to keep me supplied, man," says Lewis.

"Shit! Get stuffed, Lewis, I'm not a complete tosser," I say. "I'm not shipping any dope in here, man."

"Chocolate, arse face! I'm talking these." He rams the empty pack under my nose, "It's the least you can do for a mate who's kept you on the straight and narrow, man."

I grin. "Yes, right!" I say, and we both know, I'm the watcher.

"It stinks, man," confesses Lewis. "It's going to be a long, hard stretch for me when you're gone."

"Yeah, you're solid. You'll sail through. Just put on your pinny and get cooking, Nigella, baby." I brace for the thump, but he laughs.

He's got a lifeline now. On the outside, I'll be around, waiting. He's been a good friend.

Amy knocks on the door.

He eyes Lewis and fingers an, 'I'm watching you'.

"Come on, your carriage awaits," he says, then cruises off.

It's time. It's weird as I stand up ready to go back to my own wing. I feel gutted and scared.

I swallow hard.

We shake hands, like real grown-ups.

"See you, man," says Lewis and I can see he's hurting.

"You will. Digs, man, I'll get them sorted." I point my finger, definite.

"Yeah, do it."

I turn and walk down the corridor and off his wing. I hope I'll see Lewis again. I plan to. But that's something I've learnt in here. The future's fragile, unpredictable; it all depends on how those scales tip.

CHAPTER 27

"Taxi's here, short arse." Amy taps on my door. I pick up my large rucksack. It's heavy, but I don't have a lot of kit. I'm not the clotheshorse type. My bag's full of Harrie's letters. Three years' worth bundled up in HMYOI elastic bands. I'd spent the few days following Walter's little meltdown sorting the whole lot back into chronological order. It was a painful process purely due to the fact that I didn't have a clue why I was doing it; I could have just tossed the lot. Come to think of it, why the shit didn't I?

"Hold on, sunshine," Amy says as I go to the door. Penny and for Christ's sake, Pevensey lands up. Pevensey shoves a package in my hand. "Go on handsome, open it." Her crinkled blue eyes sparkle. I stand and gaze at it for a moment, wondering what the f***?

My cheeks flush. I focus on the wrapper, not wanting to look at the expectant eyes focusing on me. I tear off the wrapper and glance up at a circle of smiles.

I pull out a large bright red piece of cloth bag and when it falls open, it transforms into an oversize laundry bag covered in blue friggin robots.

I laugh. I feel like I'm five years old again. But the coolest thing is, some idiot's embroidered the words, Lawrence – Stay Clean.

It's the neatest laundry bag I've ever seen. They can see by the look of delight on my surprised face, I'm thinking it's one of the nicest gifts I've ever received, right up.

"Hey, that's awesome, that's really neat, guys," I say and I know I'm sounding like a five-year-old at Christmas, I just can't help myself.

"Pevensey stitched the logo," says Penny. "I can't sew for peanuts."

"And the sentiment stands, Lawrence. We like you – but we don't want to see your ugly face back in this place ever again, get it?" says Amy.

I nod. I feel a lump in my throat. I never realised how the people standing in front of me had become the substance, glueing together the pieces of my daily life. So, when the hell did I get fond of the bosses, the uniforms? I'm looking at them now in consternation. But they seem to get why.

"No returns. You can write though, if you like, let us know how it's going," says Amy and I reckon he means it.

I think of L. James and the post room. I've spent the last twelve months working in there next to the mad military and I made a lucky escape out of his plans to conscript me into the forces. A wave of disappointment washes over me. L. James isn't here for me to say goodbye and thanks. But he left word that his wife needed him to nurse her at home and sent in a good luck card.

The cloud comes back, that old nagging feeling that gives me a low. My smile fades. I feel I don't merit any of the good vibe, the positive feelings from these guys.

BALANCE

The words tumble out, clumsily, stammering back the emotion and confusion, "Thanks, so much."

Amy holds out and I shake his hand, "Pleasure. Take care."

So I'm outside and in the taxi, the engine's running while the driver, tick, ticks all the docs at the box before he transports me to the train station.

I relax back in my seat and enjoy the hum of the engine, no growling prison transport.

I look across at the white chapel building attached to the complex. My gut twists as a picture of Amar comes to mind. If he'd been here? Yeah, he'd have been surfing down the corridor to my room with his pass. He'd saunter in, his Aladdins scuffing on the floor, his hair knotted up and he'd be smiling the warmth to me. He'd demand, "Lawrence, you lovely boy, when you're out I want this, this, this and frickin this..."

He never made it.

I feel a sting in my eyes. I rub it back and look away from the chapel to the main complex.

I take myself on a virtual tour; I walk down the corridors, hear shouts and metal bolts, doors slamming, echoes drifting up, laughter, music. I'm in the observation room. Then I shift and tidy shit in my own room, sorting the letters, making the bed, colour-coding the bands, I'm in the canteen pissing about with Lewis, tossing mash at Vian or sitting by some newbie kid who's lost, gazing out.

I'm queuing for the laundry, flirting with the hula Pevensey while she tosses me a pack of wine gums as a bonus. Then it's over in classes, art, pottery, English. I'm hanging about in the exercise court watching the matches, kicking the ball back into field, lighting up Shaved's baccy with Lewis. Then my mind takes me down to the showers, in the rec room, into the guest room and I think of Mum's last visit. It was the best I'd ever had. Over in careers where the offices smell of coffee, normality.

Cabbie's in, belting up. "All right? Anyone'd think I was taking the crown jewels," he jokes and I reckon this run's a usual for the guy.

"Yeah, all good," I say.

Now we're driving out of the gates and I look back at where I've been for three years and I swear no *lie*, I'm never fucking coming back.

CHAPTER 28

From the train, I head to the police station. Not because I have to book in. No way, man. I'm free. I've served my time. No, I'm warped, got a macabre desire to do it – because I don't have to.

That's the beauty of freedom, it's all about choice. I sit on the wall and remember myself a few weeks ago, property of HMP. I think about the day I went to careers and got the sweats just by walking down the street. A panic surges, then fades at the thought of that feeling, that vertigo coming back.

A few coppers give me the eye as they wander up the steps and in and out and I smile back. I smile, man.

I shove my rucksack over my shoulder and take a walk towards the river. My room, the one that social has organized, is somewhere close by. I'm on route to drop off my kit, then I'm going to the hospital.

Shit! I can't believe Mum is still lying, trapped in a body sustained by beepers in a place that's going nowhere.

I shake the thought out of my head. At least now I can go and see her whenever I like. Now I'm here; I'm out, I'll make sure she knows it, I'll visit her every day and tell her just what I'm doing.

KIT WHITE

I've got an interview set up with the local newspaper. It's all good: local businesses take ex-offenders on a special programme and it seems the editors took a fancy to my writing style. I feel kind of bad, because I opted out of English Lit classes a few weeks before release. They filled a gap, helped me through the weeks and months, but closer to the out, life got too complicated.

But careers must have sent my work and reports from Miss Hayden to the newspaper, which meant they accepted me on to the scheme. Services said I'd probably run the coffee and copying rounds for the next five years, but when you weigh things up? It's a job and it's a tip on the upward scales of my life.

When I walk into my digs I'm shattered. The room is crap, seriously. My cell's cleaner and brighter than this dump. I put the light on only to reflect a glum, yellow shithole. Some local landlord's plastered over a condemned building and bribed the local council for a licence to let, because this place should be bulldozed. I toss my bag on to the bed in contempt. The room reeks. I look out of the tiny back window down on to the courtyard. It's been turned into a scrapyard. There's an old cracked toilet seat and sink dumped out there, obviously removed from one of the other more up-to-date residences here.

I stand and gaze around, then give myself an emotional kick up the arse. I've got to man up, face my new life, the new reality outside of Hendbrook. I'm an ex-con. What do I deserve?

A second chance!

Everyone deserves that, man.

BALANCE

I escape the slum and head down towards the hospital. It's early afternoon. The sun's warm, the streets and windows are glistening after a brief flash of rain. The world smells fresh, clean.

The doors swish open and I'm there, tripping up the steps two at a time, the bounce back because I'm free to visit Mum whenever I like.

I stride on to the ICU ward and make my way to Mum's side room. I stand, gawping like some lost kid. Her bed's empty. She's gone.

My eyes are darting around the ward, looking for someone, someone to tell me when it happened. When did mum die? I clench my fists. I'm angry. Why hadn't anyone told me? It must have been when I was on transport, it happened when I was on the train.

I stand, unable to process what's just happened. She's lost the battle. She's gone. I can't move. I'm standing in the middle of the corridor looking at her bed and I don't know which way to go. I stare at the other patients, hoping they've moved her bed. But no.

Someone knocks into my shoulder, some charge nurse. "My mum," I say, "Where..."

"S'cuse, gotta get through," he says, head down, eyes focused on the door. He shunts on, irritated as shit at my obstruction.

But I'm rigid, fixed right in the middle of the corridor; my heart's pumping, yet I'm going nowhere.

Someone's floating over; I see a figure coming towards me from a side room. It's a nurse.

I turn to her. "My mum, she was here."

The nurse recognises me. "Ah yes. Your mother's been moved on to the acute stroke unit."

A shot of relief sets me to action. "Is she better? Is she awake, now?"

She purses her lips and shakes her head. "No, I'm sorry, no change. But we've got her stabilized. They're better equipped for long-term stroke patients on the ward."

I head through the corridors, slamming back the doors, thump – in my frustration that Mum's being carted about on their trolleys, this way, that way, alive, dead, maybe, should be, not now.

When I get to the stroke unit, I find Mum right in the centre of the main ward. She's lying, pinned between two other beds, two other sleeper beepers. She's like a manikin: her skin's turned to yellow plastic, shining, unnatural. Only now the tubes are going into her arm instead of her hand. The ward's full of other stroke patients, some awake, others in a real bad way. I pull up a chair and look at her. She seems more at peace, now. Her face has changed, the lines and strange distortion have eased. Or maybe it's just that I'm suddenly more at ease.

I see my posy, the one I sent from the prison. It's in a small glass vase, my card neatly placed on the cabinet next to it. But the flowers are brown, dead, dry, no one's thrown them out. The posy's right beside her bed with the fresh blooms from Dad and Harrie carefully positioned behind it.

Then I hear her voice.

She's saying my name and I'm looking down at the floor, unable to stop the waves of emotion sweeping through my body.

BALANCE

"Lawrence."

"Lawrence, it's me."

I turn round and look up.

Harrie!

I stand, slowly. I'm trapped: pinned down, no way out.

There was so much I wanted to say, so much hurt I wanted to inflict on her and when I see her face... She's just like Mum. She has that softness, that wistful, faraway look in her eyes.

Three years. Three years.

"Harrie." I clear my throat and hover by the chair.

She smiles. "She's still here, still fighting," she says, looking down at Mum.

"Yes." I push the chair back and edge my way out. I'm panicking, gripping the chair, not letting go, but I tell her, "I'm heading off."

"I knew you'd be here today. I saw Mum this morning. It's you I've come to see, Lawrence," she says.

"I'm busy."

I want to disappear or I don't know what will happen.

I can feel my heart pounding, the heat rising, rushing through my veins as my face burns.

"We need to talk, Lawrence. We can't go on like this, not either of us." Harrie's looking at me, then Mum. "We need to do this for her. We need to do it for Mum."

"Are you taking the piss, Harrie? Are you seriously saying that to me?" I hiss. "What you did to me destroyed Mum." I'm shaking my head in disbelief at her hypocrisy.

A nurse is glancing over, frowning at the aggro that's building next to Mum's bed.

"Not here, not here, Lawrence."

"Three shitting years?" I snap.

I release the chair and look around the ward.

"Please."

I follow Harrie down the corridors like I'm her six-year-old brother again. Harrie's back, ordering me around, directing me and I'm on automatic; not seeing, just doing.

We get to the exit and we're out in the sunshine. She won't turn back to look at me. She's just leading on, determined to get me away from the hospital. She's seen a small grassy knoll across from the exit. Silently she heads over.

Then we're standing face to face and suddenly it's all there, the days, the nights, the screams and the anger and I don't waste a moment. I confront her. I know when it's done I'll be ready to turn my back on her, walk away. I'll tear her lies to pieces and make sure she'll spend the rest of her life fighting to fit it all together again.

"You sent me down, Harrie. You sent me down!" I look at her and ask her the question I've spent the last three years of my life grappling with, trying to come to terms with over and over again.

"Why did you lie to the police? Why did you tell them I pushed Rich over the side? Why?"

I'm clenching my fists, my jaw. My whole body is painfully locked in a vice.

"You know I didn't push Rich. You were there, Harrie. I saw you on the rooftop. I was high, but I saw you." My voice rises with each truth.

I have to make her understand that I know what she's done.

"Don't think I didn't. I heard you up there on the rooftop. I never pushed Rich. He hit me. I was ducking and diving from *him*. I'd never hurt Rich, never."

I'm trembling, and I can't stop myself.

"Lawrence. Rich was trying to talk you down. Trying to reason with you. But you wouldn't listen. He begged you to stop doing the tricks. He pleaded. You were high, out of it and all over the place – so close to the edge. He grabbed you and tried to drag you back. But when you broke free – that's when he tried to knock you out. He wanted to save you."

"But he went for me, he fell when I ducked. He fell. I never touched him. There was no attempted, no GBH. It was an accident."

"I know. For Christ's sake, Lawrence. How the hell could I forget? I watched him reach out, claw at the air, grasp at nothing, noone. I couldn't save him Lawrence, I was too far away... he went. It was horrific, horrific."

Harrie's putting her hands to her eyes to block out the memory: to escape from me. But I won't let her.

"Then why? Why did you lie?"

She's clenching her fists; her body's shaking. Then she slowly looks at me with renewed defiance. "You might as well have pushed him. Rich wouldn't have gone on to the roof, he wouldn't have put his life at risk if it hadn't been for you. You and your stupidity. Your senselessness. You never gave a shit, Lawrence." She's looking at me, her eyes filling with disgust.

She wants me to see her intent, that sending me down for GBH was some kind of macabre justice she'd meted out: balanced her crooked scales.

"You fucking lied!" I shout.

"Fuck, yes. Because you were losing it. On your way to killing yourself with the shit you were taking. Nobody could stop you. Nobody! And Mum, she struggled with you... She..."

"Don't say it, Harrie. Don't say that Mum's up in that bed because of me. Don't even go there," I hiss.

I side-step, I'm done. It's time for me to take off. My body's burning with rage and it's agony.

Harrie grabs my sleeve. She clutches my arm tight.

"No, Lawrence. You've had three years inside. I've had three years of letters, pleading, desperate to see this to the end. I'm not letting you walk away from this."

I jolt my arm free. My face is contorted with hate and pain but she keeps at me.

"The days and nights Mum walked the floor, sat by the phone, waited, wondering if you'd come back high or low, dead or alive," she cries. She shoves me back into the hedge, her eyes wild. "And me? What did you think I was doing when you were out on your raves? What, Lawrence?"

We're locked together, seized by the past as it tears us both to pieces. I can see it in Harrie's eyes, the desperation, the dread.

"I could have told the truth. But if I did... You would have been released within a day. No problem Lawrence, not for you. But fucking yes, for me. You just destroyed everything around you and you had no idea. You were killing yourself. It was insane. I needed to save your life too, Lawrence."

"You're the crazy, Harrie. What part of giving someone a criminal record saves a life? Eh? What part? You betrayed me." I felt my whole body tremble, "You committed perjury.

You stood up in that court and called me. It wasn't meant to happen, he was never meant to be there. You sent him after me. It's all your fucking fault."

I began laughing, laughing in disbelief at her distorted logic.

She stiffens up, her eyes wide, searching.

"Don't you get it? When you sent me down you turned me into a criminal. I don't know if I'll ever find my way back from what you've done. And I don't know why – except that you're insane," I shout.

People are walking by, staring anxiously in our direction. They quicken their pace to flee the toxic cloud that's rising between us.

Suddenly Harrie's there. I can see it as the tears flood down her cheeks, pouring out her defeat her truth.

"I hated you. I hated you. All you did was hurt. You hurt Mum, you hurt me and then – oh my God! Rich! I loved him. I loved him so much. He was such an amazing guy. He cared. He cared about me, about us. When I saw him fall. Then out on that street, in the blood, the mess, you – did – that. You took him away," she screams, her words, piercing the air and through my skull.

She walks away, stands and looks up at the sky.

I think she's going. I stand and hope.

Then she turns and walks slowly back. She takes in a deep breath.

"You see, Lawrence, it all made sense back then. I knew what I had to do, because you caused it all. You destroyed so much and you, I loved you, but..." Harrie stops, her eyes search mine.

I turn away. I can't face her.

I'd spent three years knowing this, that Harrie was the truth.

Images, reflections of what I was fill my head. I have nowhere to go.

I put my head down, fighting for breath, suffocating as the guilt and acceptance flood in. I feel the tears carrying all the loneliness, all the hurt from her betrayal.

Yet. I understand. I guess I'd always understood. But, I needed to hear it; I needed her to say those words.

I feel her wrap her arms around me and hold me tight. "Please, my brother, forgive me. I love you. Forgive me."

She rests her head on my back and sobs.

I turn and cling to her. "Harrie."

EPILOGUE

Dear Lewis,

So this is it, your lucky day.

Sorry, mate, I know it's been a few weeks. I remember, on the inside, weeks turn to months.

Get this! Those letters you always gave me grief about? We tossed them on a bonfire last night. I sat with Harrie and we watched her letters go up in a blast. Three years of writing took three minutes to turn to ashes.

It was a clear night and we were out in her back yard. It was weird, kind of cathartic for me and her.

Liberating.

I drank a can, sat on the wall next to her and watched those browns turn to white ash and float up to the sky.

Surreal.

L. James'd be foaming at the mouth.

I know, you think I'm crazy, and now you'll reckon my big sis is crazy too. Fair dos.

So, today I took my baby nephew, Vavaan, for a walk. His name's actually Vavaan Lawrence. Harrie's got a son. I couldn't believe it when I found out. Seems uni went arse up some time after I was sent down. Her grades nose-dived. But she's got a safe bloke, his name's Sai. He was in his final year at Durham when Harrie sent him all a flutter. Sai's clever as shit, he's got a degree in computer science and it's unnerving, man, but he's got the same eyes as Amar. He kind of has that warm, wise look about him, you know? I can relate to him. Yes, I can hear you calling me a soft shit. Maybe I am. Anyway, he wants Harrie to go back and finish her degree. She reckons she's not ready yet, what with Mum and Vavaan Lawrence.

But, she's gone marshmallow on Vavaan Lawrence; he is beautiful. He just laughs all the time. Sure, he does other gross baby things too, but he's freakin happy, soaking up his new life, like, everything's amazing to him.

Me? I'm in this weird place, in my head. Forgiveness, yeah? Forgiveness. I didn't know the real meaning of the word until I had to try and act it out. Go for it. It's hard as shit. But me and Harrie, we're working to get those pieces picked up and back together.

Mum's still in the stroke unit. I go every evening now I'm working at the Local Daily. I don't see the old man any more outside of a chance meeting at the hospital. I'm still angry with him. But it's kind of lessening. Like, he's hurting and yeah, he's trying. Maybe, one day.

But yesterday, I was walking Vavaan Lawrence through the park. Yeah, get me with a buggy!

The park was full, people were chilled, cruising around. Me, and Vavaan, we drifted down to the pond. The sun was powerful, shooting rays through the trees and glinting on the surface of the water. It kind of reminded me of something — that light, those colours, streaming through the break in the cloud. It reminded me of something I'd seen a lifetime ago, sitting in the canteen with you. Something I'll never forget.

My digs were the pits. But Harrie and Sai have set me up in the small room at the back of their house. I tell you, it's the best room in the world. I hit the pillow and I'm gone these nights.

It's OK working on the paper. But if you've got a record, it kind of changes how people are towards you, well the ones sniffing your history. Staff don't leave anything out that you can see, like thieving's every ex-offender's style. Guess I just have to suck it up. Harrie says it'll get easier in time. Who knows? When you're due release, Sai's going to do some flat hunting with me, try and find us digs up North. He's a safe guy.

I'm hanging around with Ellie, she's class, man, sound. She knows me, knows my history and hey, she's still hanging around. Crazy or what? She's into biking, but the serious stuff; she's making me do these road trips and pushing me to hit forty miles a day.

When my arse is burning she says, "Stop moaning, the
bicycle is the noblest invention of mankind," that's
William Saroyan, I can tell you that because she
keeps fricking telling me. She works on the paper,
comes up with all these quotes.
Yeah! I see you laughing. First time I did it, I
walked like some friggin cowboy for a week.

I would visit, but I'm not ready to come back man. Sorry! I often think of L. James, Amy and the others. They're OK for wardens. But I'm not ready to revisit all that.

When I came out, man, I thought there was nothing I'd take with me, but there is, Amar – I'll never forget him. Guess I was lucky that I had the chance to meet the guy.

Yeah! That's your monthly news digest from this daily boy. If you want the full subscription with discount and Dune bars, get off your arse and write me back.

'Till then, my friend – enjoy the chocolate I've sent. There's a whole load more coming your way.

Keep up the cooking, Nigella.

Keep those scales balanced, man.

Lawrence

END

FURTHER INFORMATION

http://www.drugwise.org.uk/
Promoting evidence-based information on drugs, alcohol and tobacco.

http://www.talktofrank.com/need-support
Search for local services in your area on the link above.

http://www.nta.nhs.uk/uploads/nta_getting_help_with_a_drug_problem.pdf
The National Treatment Agency for Substance Misuse

http://www.familylives.org.uk/about/our-services/action-for-prisoners-and-offenders-families/
Action for Prisoners and Offender's Families

http://www.adfam.org.uk/
Improving support for families affected by drugs and alcohol.

Printed in Great Britain
by Amazon